For the Love of Lisa

Callie Norse

Carafe Publishing

For the Love of Lisa

ISBN-13: 978-0692739778
ISBN-10: 0692739777

Acknowledgments

I would like to thank those who have continually supported me in my writing. To each of my select few friends, who I have allowed to read the book, I owe huge thanks. The overwhelming enthusiasm you have shown for this book and my writing, has given me much encouragement to continue on with my writing and to publish. Many times, when I have doubted myself, your words have enabled me to continue. Thank-you Martha, Anna, and Wanda.

I also wish to thank my husband for his support and encouragement to publish this book.

Excerpt from For the Love of Lisa

Lisa made herself a salad and sat to relax a few minutes before changing clothes. She ate in the sewing room, so if Greg walked in he wouldn't see her eating. He would be curious as to why she was eating, when he thought she had just come from a lunch date. Looking at her mom's rocker in the sewing room made her think of when Maggie was a baby. Everything reminded her of babies these days. She was continuing to dream of a baby crying. It must be because of her desire to have another baby, she had decided. The dreams increased her desire. She was puzzled as to why the baby's cry sounded troubled. She hoped this didn't mean there would be something wrong with her baby. She would be glad when Dr. Fontell called confirming her pregnancy.

After lunch, Lisa went upstairs to change clothes, exhausted from her trip to the doctor. The bed looked inviting. She stretched across the queen-size canopy bed and was fast asleep within minutes.

She awoke with Greg's kiss on the lips. "Sleepy gal, again today, I see." Lisa stirred enough to return his kiss. "Amy and her mom came by and asked to take Maggie to the afternoon matinee. I thought it would be good for her to spend some time with Amy. She hasn't been with anyone her age for a few weeks. And you know how much she has wanted to see Shrek 2. I knew you would agree, so I let her go. I had her wash up and change into some clean clothes. She put on her purple shorts and the little lavender shirt. I called the shirt purple. She was quick to correct me that it's lavender. You girls are so particular about such things."

Lisa looked up at him and smiled. "Are you finished with your gardening for the day?"

"I could be if you would like me to be," he grinned.

"I was thinking maybe we could spend some quality time in the Jacuzzi while Maggie is away."

"Amazing how we think alike. First, I think it would be a good idea if I wash off in the shower," Greg answered.

Lisa agreed. She was dressed in only a half-slip, bra, and panties—all light green, a Martha Stewart green, as Greg called it. Greg cupped his hand inside her bra, exposing a breast. He lowered his lips to the nipple and began to suck, as he couldn't resist the temptation. He loved her breasts and knew this would get her going. It always did.

"Honey, if you ever want to make it to the Jacuzzi, you'd better quit that, or we will be making love right here on the bed, with you in your dirty clothes."

He gave her a peck on the lips, as he tucked her breast back inside her bra, and gave her well-filled bra cup a soft pat. He then disappeared into the new adjoining bath. Lisa arrived as he was stepping out of his sexy black briefs, which never failed to excite her. They fit just snugly enough to show the outline of his arousal, which she took in her hand. She so loved to feel his progression, which now already had a head start. He reached around her; his fingers feeling for her bra hooks. One by one he unfastened them allowing her bra to drop to the floor, exposing her amazing breasts. He slowly slid her half-slip down her legs, leaving only her bikini panties, which he eased off her sexy ass and down her shapely thighs.

Her heart began racing as he spread her thighs. His fingers became playful.

Lisa then worried he would detect the lubricant Dr. Fontell used for the exam. "Greg honey, we need to get the Jacuzzi ready. Why don't you take your shower while I run the water?" She turned on the gold plated faucet and added a few drops of the gardenia-scented bath salts, which Greg had given her as a surprise the day the Jacuzzi was completed. He lit the floating candles surrounding the tub, turned on soft music, and closed the shutters on the window to block the outside light. The room was now a perfect romantic setting. The tub had finished filling by the time Greg stepped out of the shower. Lisa could see he was quite ready! She handed him some wine from the small refrigerator they had filled with wine and chilled glasses. He popped the cork and poured two glasses while she held them.

Days earlier, Lisa had replaced their usual wine with non-alcoholic wine, suspecting she might be pregnant. She gave Greg the excuse it would be less tiring since she was still adjusting to the added responsibilities of the new house. He took the filled glasses from her and sat them on the ledge alongside the Jacuzzi, then took her hand to help her in, admiring her beauty, as always. The warm bubbling water with the floral scent felt quite relaxing. Greg handed Lisa one of the glasses of wine and took the other for himself. They sipped their wine as they relaxed listening to "Let's Make Love" by Faith Hill and Tim McGraw. Greg leaned in and kissed Lisa, immediately causing her to respond. She was now feeling in a much more romantic mood than she had been in for weeks.

The kiss went on and on. Lisa orgasmed. Greg

could never understand how she did this. He began fondling her delicious breasts. As he sucked on her erect nipples, first one, then the other, her body arched toward him. He reached into the water, feeling, massaging, and exciting her even more. She knelt over top of him, lowering herself onto him. She loved the feeling. His size was more than she could have ever dreamed of. She began to rhythmically ride him, first slowly, then faster as pleasures mounted. Suddenly, she came down hard on him. Water splashed and ran out onto the floor. They hardly noticed.

Greg became more vocal. Lisa was close to being out of control. They loved it when they became this involved. They reached their peak at the same moment. Greg lifted her out of the water and carried her into the bedroom, where they lay cuddling until sleep came.

One

On a dreary March day, Greg and Lisa Carrington and their six-year-old daughter, Maggie, sat snugly in the living room of their small apartment, watching television and listening to the rain. With each drop, the once beautiful snow melted, washing down the hillside and emptying into the city drainage system.

The small town of Galena, Illinois, was a tourist town known for its beautiful older hillside homes and for skiing at the nearby resort of Chestnut Mountain. For this reason, it was always sad to see the snow begin to melt. Greg and Lisa had grown up with the love of skiing. They had first taken Maggie to learn the art at the age of four. After many spills, she learned to stay on her feet with the red plastic skis Santa had given her for Christmas that year. She was doing quite well for such a young age, which was not unusual for children of Galena. Soon she would be ready to move up from the beginner slope where she had spent many hours

The phone rang. Greg reached over to the table beside his recliner and picked up the handset. Lisa looked on, admiring how handsome he was in his red lambskin shirt, with a black turtleneck exposed at the neckline. Red was the perfect contrast to his dark brown hair, which he always kept neatly cut across the nape of his neck, with a loose-combed look on top. His deep brown eyes, which sparkled as he spoke, and his prominent dimples, made him irresistible to Lisa from the start—not to mention his muscular physique. He lacked the height to be described as tall, dark, and handsome, for he stood only five foot nine. Lisa considered herself quite fortunate to have a husband so handsome; however, this wasn't her top priority in a man. His personality always stood out to her. He put other people's needs above his. He was always there to help those who needed help, no matter what it was.

For Lisa it was love at first sight. The moment he spoke to her in geometry class, she knew he was the one. He sat directly across the aisle from her. She often caught him glancing over at her. Two weeks into the school year, he had invited her to a movie. They hit it off so well they began dating on a regular basis. After a few months, she became his steady girl. She felt proud to be Greg's girl. He could have had any girl he wanted. He was the guy all the girls swooned over—he chose her. This made her feel quite special.

Greg was every bit as proud to be her guy. At first glance, he noticed her beautiful blue eyes that glistened as she spoke, her smile being equally as warm. She wore her shoulder length, ash brown hair flipped under slightly at the ends, with short wispy, swoop bangs. Lisa, a mere five foot three, weighed only one hundred ten pounds. She carried herself in a manner that made her clothes look expensive, even when they were not. Of course, it helped that all the curves were in the right places. Greg was continuously trying to catch a glimpse of her breasts, as she reached under her desk to lay her books on the rack under the chair seat. What guy wouldn't? He loved it when she wore blouses that were slightly low cut—not so low they were sexy, only slightly revealing in certain positions. Occasionally, there would be a gap between her blouse and her breasts allowing him to see her cleavage and the firm rounded top of her breasts, which caused a desire he tried not to dwell on—especially not in geometry class. Their love for each other deepened with each passing day.

Lisa could hear only one side of the conversation as Greg spoke, "We did? Wonderful! Fine, thanks so much for calling." She knew from his words that it was the realtor who had shown them the old, three-story, Victorian home at the edge of town. Greg placed the phone on the table, sprang up, placed his arms around Lisa's waist, and twirled her in the air. "We got it!" he shouted. They had put a bid in for the marvelous old house they had fallen in love with, even before the realtor had taken them through it. Having been on the market for a while, they had hoped the owners would accept their moderate bid, which they had. They now could move out of their tiny, cramped apartment in the center of town.

They married while Greg was attending college, studying to be an accountant. Lisa was studying interior design. Greg was hired part time at a local firm before graduating. It was a small company at the time. Now Barker and Ream was the largest firm in the area. Greg loved his work, and was a hard worker. He had moved up the corporate ladder quite quickly. By their late twenties, he and Lisa were doing much better financially than their peers.

Lisa's interior design degree and excellent taste had

assured her of many clients in the area, and now she was looking forward to designing their own dream home.

The Carringtons were ecstatic over this enchanting Victorian. They knew as soon as they stepped in the front door that the exterior hadn't misled them. This was the house they had been looking for.

The house was built in the 1870's, then remodeled and redecorated in the early 1900's. It was apparent there had been other changes made since then, making the home no longer a true Victorian. Lisa and Greg approved of these changes, as they made the house homier. They loved the large rooms with thirteen foot high ceilings. There was still much of the Victorian era remaining to make the house special.

Since touring the home, they had talked and planned as if they knew it would soon be theirs. Now they could put their ideas into effect. The first floor had a sitting room off the kitchen, which had a window seat. Lisa would convert this into her sewing/craft room. The cast iron fireplace in this room was typical of the era. This would be the perfect room for her mom's old wooden rocker. She had persuaded her mom to give it to her after she became pregnant with Maggie. Here she sat and rocked Maggie as a baby. It seemed the perfect chair in which to nurse her new baby and to spend time reading to her. Lisa loved reading to Maggie. She began reading to her when she was only six months old. Maybe this could partially account for Maggie's sharpness, as they had heard reading to a young baby helps develop a baby's learning abilities. Maggie had begun reading some words at the age of four.

*

The thirty-day wait before they could take possession passed quickly, while Lisa and Greg made preparations for renovating the house. Today the house would be theirs.

Maggie had waited impatiently for this day to come. Greg had no more than taken the key out of the ignition, when Maggie opened the door of the car and jumped out onto the sidewalk, stopping at the gate of the wrought iron fence enclosing the yard. As soon as Greg opened the gate, she ran up the steps to the front porch, her little legs running as fast as they could—her long, blonde, curly hair bouncing and blowing in the breeze. Here, she waited for Greg and Lisa, her little round face bursting with happiness. She looked so cute, her dimples so apparent, as she grinned from ear to ear.

Greg was so excited himself that he began to wonder if he had the right key. After much fumbling, the key turned in the lock, and they were in. Maggie was at the top of the open spiral staircase before Greg and Lisa had the door shut behind them. She had been anxious to see her room again. The large flowers on the wallpaper seemed to have grown larger since she first saw them. Lisa and Greg knew there would be no peace until the wallpaper was removed. Maggie had pondered for days over the wallpaper books Lisa had brought home. It seemed each day she had a new favorite, until finally she chose one. She loved pink—as most little girls do. Lisa had convinced her that pink tie back curtains would complement the wallpaper, which had a light background with a pink design of hearts and flowers intermingled. They had chosen pink velvet fabric for the window seat cushion.

Greg had built a window seat in his brother-in-law's home workshop, since this room had none. The large bay window was in three sections. The smaller side windows angled in toward the main window. The window seat followed the same line as the window. The carpet had been ordered—of course it was pink!

First, the wiring must be replaced. An electrician had been hired. The bathroom fixtures all had to be replaced with new—a very quaint, Victorian style to match the theme of the house. The kitchen cabinets were to be torn out. The previous owners had been kind enough to allow the cabinetmaker in to measure for the new cabinets, which were now completed and ready to be installed.

The downstairs would all be redecorated. The decorators were to come as soon as the wiring was replaced. Meanwhile there were plenty of other things to do. They loved the entire house. Lisa couldn't decide if her favorite was the grand drawing room, which was fifteen by thirty feet, the parlor with the rare pink marble fireplace, or the sitting room off the kitchen, which would be her sewing/craft room. Greg had some repairs to do on the window seat in the sewing room. The top board had split and warped with age. The original hardwood floor would remain in this room. Lisa found the perfect braided rug. On this, would sit her mom's old wooden rocker.

Lisa loved the old treadle sewing machines. Hers had to succumb to a new one, as her sewing was more complex than the old machines were capable of. She had inherited her grandmother's machine—now an antique. It was being stored in her sister's attic and would be cleaned up and moved into the family dining room. She knew the old treadle would add to the charm of the room.

The third floor would stay as it was for now until the other two floors were finished—possibly until there was a need for them. There were six bedrooms upstairs. It would take some time to fill these, two of which would be spare bedrooms for now. That would leave one for the baby they hoped to have as soon as life settled back to normalcy. They were considering using one of the others as an office for Greg. Someday the third floor could be turned into guest quarters, after they filled all the bedrooms with the children they planned to have—first things first. They had waited so long for a home like this one. Lisa wanted to be sure everything was finished to her perfection before she was slowed down with morning sickness. Maggie had been a difficult pregnancy in the first months. Lisa remembered how she envied women whose morning sickness was just that, as hers with Maggie continued all day.

Things were much different back then. Her mom was still living at that time. She had been a big help to her. Now there was no mom to help. She would manage fine—although the loss had left a void never to be replaced by anyone. It had been two years since her passing. Lisa felt she had been cheated. Twenty-five was much too young to lose a mom.

*

The big day finally came, the day when the house would become a home for the Carringtons. Maggie was up at first dawn begging for Greg to load her precious things into the van. "Daddy," she insisted, "I want to take my dollies in the car with us. They will be lonely in the big truck with the men."

"Okay, we will keep your dollies with us," he agreed, "We want them to be happy." He knew she would be persistent about this matter. After all, it was such a small thing to ask.

Maggie was at the door waiting for Greg, as he swallowed the last bite of his whole wheat bagel and washed it down with coffee. Earlier, Maggie had nibbled on toast and peanut butter. Breakfast was light and simple today, as were the appetites on this long awaited day.

"Can you believe it? This is really ours!" Greg glanced over to see Lisa's response, as he pulled into the driveway of the old carriage house, which had been converted into a garage years before. It had previously been a stable for the horses, a tack room, and a carriage room. The second floor was storage for hay for the horses, which they would throw down through a trap door. Greg was making plans for converting part of the carriage house into a workshop. He loved woodworking.

Maggie hopped out of the car and headed for the old servants' entrance at the rear of the house. She was dragging a cloth bag of toys behind her, while she sang, "Hi ho, Hi ho, it's off to work we go," from Snow White and the Seven Dwarfs.

This entrance led to the back servants' hallway, which allowed access to two stairways. The one going up led to the second floor where there was another servants' hallway. This led to the third floor, containing four bedrooms and a large sitting room that in early years were used for the female servants. This third floor mansard wasn't an attic, as the ceilings were ten feet high. The servants' hallway on the ground floor gave access to the kitchen. In this hallway, there was a washstand for the servants use. At the end of the hall, there was a door with a particularly beautiful stained glass panel.

With his arms loaded, Greg waited as Lisa unlocked the door. He carried two cardboard boxes of Maggie's dolls and other precious cargo in through the kitchen, where Lisa stopped to admire the new cabinets that replicated the original ones. They had been installed only a few days earlier. Greg chose to go up the front stairway, as the back servants' steps were steep and narrow. It would be easier to carry the boxes in through the kitchen. Besides, he was anxious to walk through the first floor rooms to take another look at all the beautiful renovations.

After placing the boxes in Maggie's room, he left her to unpack her toys. She busied herself filling the window seat with many of her toys. Then, one by one, she placed her little dollies on the window seat, just moments before movers arrived. Her dollhouse, pink of course, and her little pink rocker were arranged to complement the room—so she thought. "Mommy said for you to put it over there," she instructed the movers with the point of a finger, as they carried in her white poster canopy bed. Once the bed was in place and her dollies were seated at the small table and chairs for a tea party, she danced down the spiral staircase to watch the movers.

Maggie's second most favorite room, the first being her bedroom, seemed to be Mommy's sewing/craft room, which also would serve as her storybook room. Numerous children's books would line the bookshelf against one wall. The window seat in this room would be filled with fabric, old and new.

There were many scraps from little outfits Lisa had made for Maggie, most of which she had now outgrown. Lisa usually managed to use most remnants for one thing or another, since she enjoyed making craft items and doll clothes for Maggie's dolls—and there was always mending. Lisa felt this room had a particular air of comfort. She wasn't sure what it was that made it so special. Maybe it was the cast iron fireplace, or visions of the room once all other furnishings were placed in the room. Lisa was sure they would quickly feel very much at home in this room.

For now, there was much to be done. There were beds to make and a large number of boxes to unpack. Each room now contained multiple boxes, all neatly labeled with the contents. Each was marked with the room in which the movers were to place it. Lisa had done all she could to make this move an easier transition.

By nightfall, the three of them were exhausted. The furniture had all been arranged and rearranged at least once. The boxes, one by one, were unpacked until there now were many less than earlier in the day. Maggie moved from one room to another, excited and giggling, while she watched with constant smiles. It was easy to tell how much she already loved this big house.

Greg started a fire in the fireplace in the parlor. Lisa arranged some large pillows on the floor in front of the fire. They all sprawled out cozily on the floor, their stomachs warm with the chili Lisa had prepared at the apartment the day before. She had known this was to be a hectic day with little time for meal preparation. What a beautiful picture this would make—the three of them in front of the elegant pink marble fireplace. No wonder Maggie loved this house, as there were touches of pink marble throughout.

"This is the bestest house in the whole world," Maggie yawned. Within minutes she was fast asleep, snuggled in between Greg and Lisa.

Greg picked her up and carried her upstairs to her bed. He couldn't help notice, as he placed her in bed, how all of her little dolls were laid in a row on the pink velvet window seat. They were covered with various little blankets, with the clothes they had been wearing placed on the seat beside them. He didn't peek under the blankets—he knew they were all wearing either nightgowns or pajamas, which Lisa had made.

When he returned, Lisa had two glasses of wine on the marble hearth. "I thought we could use a little something to help us relax," she whispered softly, as she gave Greg that special look, look he knew. Lisa was a gentle, passionate lady. The original spark between her and Greg was still there. Greg lay down beside her, and handed her a glass of wine, taking the other for himself. They sipped their wine while enjoying the glowing fire. They talked of all they had accomplished throughout the day, and how pleased they were with the house and all its features.

When Lisa emptied her wine glass, she set it on the hearth, and lay down beside Greg. Her hair was a bit mussed, she wore no makeup, and was dressed in blue jeans and a simple cotton t-shirt. To Greg, she was still the most beautiful gal in the world. He kissed her neck and nibbled on her ear, which brought a smile as she leaned over to kiss him. The first kiss, which began soft and tender, quickly set the mood. Piece by piece they removed each other's clothing. The glow of the fire sent a flickering, golden glow across their naked bodies as they made love. This, the perfect physical joining of a couple in love, was a very important part of their marriage. Their love grew and blossomed with each day. There was never a harsh word between them. The tenderness and kindness came natural for them. They truly had a wonderful love.

It had been a long, busy day, and it felt good to relax in each other's arms by the warmth of the fire. They lay there for hours occasionally dozing off. Lisa suddenly awoke from a dream, to the sound of a baby crying. It had to be a dream. There was no baby in the house. "Greg," she whispered in his ear. "I think we should go up to bed now."

He snuffed out the fire, rose to his feet, and helped Lisa up. He stood still for a few seconds, as if he was listening, before going toward the spiral staircase. They again admired the grand drawing room as they walked through.

The bedroom was quite large. Boxes were piled everywhere. This bedroom had the original marble washstand with both hot and cold running water, which most of the bedrooms originally had. Lisa was pleased that this one remained, as it added to the Victorian look. Many of the Victorian touches were now gone. The beautiful hardwood floor in this master bedroom was the original floor, which they had refinished. At first they had doubts whether it could be restored to be worthwhile. They were extremely pleased with the end results. It looked almost as it must have originally, except for a slight discoloration.

The original cast iron fireplace had been replaced with one of Italian tile mosaic, with a fireplace screen of rosewood, inset with panels of embroidered silk. The ceiling was molded plaster in the Italian style. The walls were repapered with rose damask. There were wooden cornices of burled walnut with gold inlay above the windows. Interior shutters were installed here and throughout the house, when the house was built. They appeared to be in reasonably good shape.

Lisa had chosen a bed cover that replicated the rose damask wall covering. This room was also a favorite of hers. She removed the beautiful bed cover, and placed it on a Victorian quilt stand she had found in a local antique shop. She folded the bed covers back and slipped in between the ivory sheets, with the delicate rosewood embroidery decorating the top casing. With Greg watching her every movement, thinking how beautiful her body was, he slipped into bed beside her. He knew he was an extremely lucky guy to have found a love like he had with Lisa. Her inner beauty equally matched her outer beauty. They lay in one another's arms and soon fell asleep, feeling ever so loved.

Morning came all too quickly. After their morning shower, Lisa went down the back staircase to the kitchen. Passing by Maggie's room, she noticed Maggie's dollies were still fast asleep on the window seat. Maggie was beginning to stir. As Lisa started down the back stairs, she got a whiff of baby powder. *How can this be? It must be a psychological reaction to last night's dream.*

As Greg approached the back stairs, he was deep in thought trying to decide which of the remaining bedrooms to use as his office. With time so limited, only two of the bedrooms had been redecorated so far. Now the plans could begin for the other four upstairs rooms. Lisa had suggested tearing out the back wall of their bedroom closet. This could open into an adjoining bath with a Jacuzzi and walk in closet. It would break the Victorian theme, but it would add some romantic charm, which was very important to both of them. Greg decided the room at the far end of the hall might best serve as his office. It was far from the other bedrooms now being used and close to the back stairs, where he could easily slip down to the kitchen or out the servants' entry to the carriage house.

By now, he could hear Maggie moving about in her room—more than likely, waking her babies and dressing them for the day. In the kitchen below, he could hear Lisa preparing breakfast. He stood in the center of this back room trying to decide how to decorate his office, when he heard Maggie instructing her dollies as she was leaving her bedroom to take the spiral staircase down to the kitchen, "Now eat all your breakfast, and be good little children." She preferred to take the long way to the kitchen to get another look at the grand drawing room. She peeked into each room as she strutted through the large house, which she loved more with each passing minute. She appeared in the kitchen wearing her favorite little jeans and cute pink shirt, which she had persuaded Lisa to buy for her, saying it would be her new house shirt. On the front of the shirt, there was a large heart with a smiley face inside the heart. She had begged, "This makes me think of how our new house will make my heart happy."

Greg could smell the sausage from the top of the stairs. He entered the kitchen while Lisa was flipping the last pancake onto the serving platter. Maggie was placing the silverware beside each plate—there being nothing consistent about where she placed them. No place setting was identical, although each had the necessary pieces. Greg grabbed two coffee mugs and poured coffee for the two of them. Lisa poured a small glass of white milk for Maggie. Chocolate was Maggie's choice. This, she was allowed only occasionally.

No one was in any rush today. Greg had taken the day off to help unpack. They sat around the table in the family dining room discussing where to put what. There were many boxes to unpack yet. They now wondered how they had managed to store all these things in one small apartment. They had known it was crowded but hadn't realized quite how much they had packed into such little space.

After breakfast, Greg helped Lisa with the dishes. They enjoyed small conversation until Maggie wandered off to the sewing/craft room. Being alone with Lisa made Greg want to enjoy her to the fullest. He reached out to her as he put the last dish in the cupboard. He pressed his body close to hers as his lips met hers. Oh, those breasts! He hadn't stopped admiring them in all the years since he caught his first glimpse of them in high school. Lisa felt him swell as they embraced. There was much work to be done and Maggie was near.

Soon, Greg was back upstairs measuring for the renovations in his office, gathering ideas in his head, while Lisa went to the sewing room to check on Maggie. She was unpacking her little books and placing them on the bookshelf as she sang a little tune, "Clean up, clean up, everybody everywhere. Clean up, clean up, everybody do your share"…the Barney clean-up song. She loved watching Barney when she was younger. Her interest in Barney was now fading a bit—she was outgrowing him. The tune still stuck in her head, especially today, as she happily worked to help make this their home. As Lisa listened to her sing, she began to empty a box of fabric, placing each remnant neatly into the window seat. Each one held a special memory.

When the boxes were emptied, she stood back and

studied the round braided rug she had purchased. *Just a little more to the left will be better,* she thought, as she centered it with the cast iron fireplace. Next, she placed the wooden rocker on the rug, arranging it to her liking. This reminded her of a framed picture she had once seen in a store, and now regretted not buying it. It was one of those items you never seem to forget and always wish you had purchased. She had gone back to the store later, only to find it had been sold. The memory now enabled her to replicate the picture in her own home. Her sewing machine sat in the opposite corner of the room, where she could look across the room and see this replication. She smiled, *Yes, this is definitely the coziest room in the house.* She could tell that Maggie felt the same.

Greg was falling a little short on the unpacking. He had a moderate number of tools in boxes, which he had taken to the carriage house and left there, until he could make a decision as to which room to use for his workshop. He now found himself on the back steps headed for the carriage house to look over the tack room as a possibility. He would help Lisa unpack boxes when he returned. The carriage house was set back a ways further from the house than one would like a garage to be. The uniqueness made up for that. The tack room looked to Greg as if it could make a substantial workshop. It wasn't very large, but his tools were fairly basic and wouldn't require much room. He checked the boxes to make sure all the tools were there. Not much could be done until the house was more unpacked.

On the way back to the house, he saw a strange streak of light move across the lawn in front of him and disappear at the edge of the house by the servants' entrance. This was puzzling, to say the least. *Could this have been lightning?* There was no storm. The sky was clear for the most part, only a few white cumulous clouds—the kind that he and Lisa loved to have fun finding faces and figures in. Maggie would giggle as they pointed out each one. The carriage house was rather dark since there were few windows. *It must be my eyes adjusting to the sunlight.*

As he opened the door at the servant's entrance, he could hear giggles coming from the formal dining room. Lisa and Maggie were unpacking dishes and placing them in the buffet. "Be very careful, Maggie. These were Grandma's dishes. They are very old. They were your great grandmother's before she passed them down to Grandma."

Greg gathered up the many boxes they had already unpacked and carried them outside to burn. By the looks of all the boxes, he guessed he was gone longer than he had thought. He placed the boxes in a large burning barrel, one at a time, watched them ignite and burn rapidly, and then returned to the house.

The pantry had not yet been unpacked. Greg decided this would be a good place for him to start. It should be simple enough. There were pine cabinet doors and drawers with storage space for spices and herbs and bins for flour, meal, and sugar. He knew by now that in Lisa's kitchen, the spices and herbs were to be stored alphabetically. He proceeded to wash out the bins. Being unsure what he should put in the meal bin, he left this for Lisa to decide.

The small room at the end of the kitchen intrigued Greg. This contained an oak icebox, which in earlier years was supplied by the iceman through a small door, which opened from the outside. A servants' call box was mounted on the wall beside the kitchen door. Years back, when members of the families wanted service, they would press a bell that dropped a tab into the call box to show the servants in which room the call originated. This room definitely showed the era from which it was built.

Much time had passed by the time Greg finished investigating all the proprieties of this room. After the last spices were placed in order on the shelf, he realized the house had become silent. He first peeked into the formal dining room where he had last seen Lisa and Maggie. The room looked to be in good order, with empty boxes stacked in one corner. There was no Lisa, no Maggie. He continued toward the front of the house looking into each room. *Where could they be?* he wondered, as he stepped onto the front porch hoping to find them there. Nothing. Two baby bunnies were chasing one another through the yard. Greg didn't notice. He was too concerned as to the whereabouts of Lisa and Maggie. He quickly mounted the spiral staircase, taking the steps two at a time. There on Maggie's bed, they lay fast asleep with a book of Cinderella face down on Lisa's chest. *They have worked hard this morning,* he thought to himself, as he continued down the hall thinking this was a good opportunity to get back to his office plans. He stopped in the doorway, looking over the room, picturing his furniture in various places, and trying to decide how he wanted the finished room to look. Wainscoting on the lower portion of the walls would give the room more of an office look. "This will be my room, my present day room!" He had seen some great furniture at a local office supply store. The moment he saw it, he knew his office would be an exception to Victorian. He would paint the walls a dark blue above the wainscoting. There was much pink throughout the house. This was his room, and he planned to make just that statement. Greg did a bit more measuring, and then went back downstairs to see what boxes he could attack next.

After a while, he heard Lisa and Maggie coming down the back stairs. Lisa was soon mustering up some lunch of left over chili. They all loved chili, so no one complained about the leftovers, especially at such a busy time.

The wind began to howl as darkness crept in. The lights were flickering. This large old house seemed less cozy than it had earlier. They decided to gather in the parlor and forget about work for the evening. There would be plenty of time for that tomorrow.

Greg noticed Lisa yawning. Her nap obviously had been too short. The three of them lay on the floor, in front of the fireplace, just as they had the night before. The fireplace was comforting in the storm. Maggie babbled on about this and that until the lights would flicker. Each time, she drew her small body closer to Lisa. Lisa fell asleep long before Maggie. Greg again carried Maggie upstairs and put her into bed. He returned to find Lisa still fast asleep and no wine on the mantel. Greg so desired the romance they had shared the night before. He reached for a throw on the arm of the sofa, lay down beside Lisa and drew the blanket up over them. He lay there thinking how much Lisa meant to him and how much her love for him meant. They were so fortunate to have found their true love the first time around. Many couples never find it.

Greg missed her. His desires were strong, although he wouldn't wake her. He knew she was exhausted. The move had been more stressful for her than he had known. They would sleep there until she awoke.

When Morning came, Greg began to get uncomfortable on the floor. He got up, leaving Lisa still sleeping soundly and went to shower and change. He then began searching for the waffle iron and the waffle/pancake mix. He soon found them and began making breakfast.

The smell of coffee and waffles began filtering into the parlor, waking Lisa. She strolled out to the kitchen and wrapped her arms around Greg's neck, "What a wonderful aroma to wake up to. Thank you, honey." He drew her close. Their lips met in a kiss. As he pressed his body to hers, she felt his thickening flesh. She regretted falling asleep so quickly. "After breakfast, Maggie will be busy waking up all her dollies and feeding them breakfast," she whispered.

"I was thinking the same thing," Greg winked. "Our breakfast is ready now." They sat quietly talking, making plans for the day. One thing certainly seemed to be planned out before the first bite of waffle!

Maggie came traipsing into the kitchen, her face bright and cheery. "Did you leave any for me?" Greg got up from the table and took a glass of orange juice out of the refrigerator and put more batter in the waffle iron. She downed the juice and helped herself to the sausage on the table. As she swallowed the last bite, Greg put a waffle on the table in front of her. She talked about the dream she had. One of her babies had been crying. She assumed the storm had scared the baby. Greg and Lisa found this quite interesting.

They all went upstairs when Maggie was finished eating—Maggie to get out of her jammies and get dressed for the day and to tend to her babies. Lisa explained to her how she and Daddy had slept in front of the fireplace. Therefore, she needed to take a shower and change clothes.

Greg closed the bedroom door behind them. Finally, they were alone. Desires had been rising since before breakfast. Greg's fingers couldn't unbutton Lisa's blouse fast enough. Her C-cup bra fell to the floor exposing her luscious breasts. In her excitement, Lisa ripped Greg's shirt off—a few buttons were now missing. He leaned her back onto the bed and removed her jeans and panties. Oh, the desires… His masculine hands gently and slowly moved over her, tracing the curves of her bottom, her hips, her breasts—igniting in her a restless craving to get closer, to touch and be touched more intimately. There was little time, as Maggie would soon finish with her dollies. Greg's belt buckle clanged as his jeans hit the hardwood floor. He lay down beside Lisa, holding her curvaceous body closely, drawing his thumbs across her nipples hardening them into tight little peaks, increasing desires. He so wished there had been more time. He wanted to enjoy everything wonderful that making love meant to them. This was not the time. He slowly entered her, watching her facial expressions, and listening to her quiet moans as her passions rose, and climaxed. He loved pleasing her.

Maggie's footsteps were heard coming down the hall. Lisa grabbed a robe and headed for the shower. Greg clutched the covers and pulled them up over his nude body. Lisa and Maggie met in the hallway. "I'll be out of the shower in a minute."

Maggie entered their bedroom. "Daddy, what are you doing in bed?"

"I thought I would lie here until Mommy finished with her shower. This bed feels so good."

"I know," Maggie said, "you're being lazy. My

babies need me. They are a little fussy today." She turned and left the room.

Greg was out of bed and dressed by the time Lisa finished showering and returned to their bedroom. She approached him and put her arms around him. "Oh my, my girl wants more," he teased.

"Well, it was awfully quick you know. I love having Maggie at home with us, although at times like this I wish spring break was over." As she spoke, she drew her body closer to Greg. Oh, my! He apparently still had desires, too. It would be a long day unless Maggie napped.

Greg took Lisa's suggestion, to work on the construction plans, while she and Maggie unpacked things. It was difficult to know where she wanted everything, until she herself saw how things were fitting into the allotted spaces.

Greg returned to the empty room to ponder over the plans for the new bath. He wanted this to be a very special room—a room that would encourage romance. He decided to have the Jacuzzi partially sunken, with a ledge to set candles and fresh rose petals on occasionally. There would be a dimmer on the light switch and a mirror on the wall across from the Jacuzzi. They were including a shower in this room, even though the bath down the hall had a shower. Many times they would want a quick shower—therefore, it would be much more convenient to have one off the bedroom, than to walk down the hall to the other bath. They had ordered a Jacuzzi with a pearly luster, which they had fallen in love with the moment they saw it. The shower they found had gold trim to match the gold plated fixtures. The final touch of elegance was a lavatory with a pink marble top.

Greg finished measuring and planning. The carpenter would be there in the morning to begin the work. He had, also, agreed to do the work on the office. Greg needed the time to get his workshop together, and he couldn't see prolonging the mess in the house. He took the back stairs down to the kitchen. Lisa was arranging and rearranging, to make room for the rest of the items. They must all be perfectly arranged.

"Lisa, sweetie, I have called the carpenter. There is nothing more I can do here. I need to run downtown and order some materials for him to get started in the morning. Then I will run to the office supply store to order the furniture for my office."

"Okay, honey. Suppose you could pick up something for supper on your way home? There is so much to do here, yet."

"Sure, hon, anything in mind?"

"Pizza or lasagna from that new little place would be nice."

"I'll surprise you then," he winked.

His wink told Lisa it would be lasagna for sure. After all, it was his favorite. She would order pizza to be delivered someday soon, as she was definitely craving it."

On his way out the door, he peeked in on Maggie in the sewing room arranging her little books to her own liking. She was every bit as particular as her mommy. Her doll buggy had now made its way downstairs, and two babies were fast asleep in it. Lisa knew Maggie had conned Daddy into bringing it down for her, although she hadn't seen him carry it in.

Greg couldn't leave without first going into the tack room to take another look at what would soon be his workshop. Something urged him to go into the old stable. Strange—a red substance was on the floor, below the trap door. He squatted down and touched it. It was a sticky substance, resembling blood. He climbed the ladder and looked into the loft above. It looked perfectly normal—that is, normal for an old loft, which hadn't been used in years. Greg remained puzzled. There were some old rags in the corner, which he used to clean up the substance. He tossed the rags into an old burning barrel, behind the carriage house, and drove off in his metallic gray Tahoe, still puzzled over what he had seen.

It took only a few minutes for him to reach the office supply store. He was able to put the incident in the stable out of his mind, until he had completed his order for the office furniture with the sales lady. As soon as he got back into his Tahoe, he became so engrossed with the incident he almost forgot to pick up the lasagna, which he had ordered from his cell phone, earlier.

When he returned, Lisa and Maggie were sitting in the old wooden rocker in the sewing room, reading Snow White.

"I'm hungry, Daddy," Maggie whined. Greg noticed Lisa was somewhat pale. She was quite tired and ate very little. He cleaned up the dishes and told her to rest. He was afraid she had overdone.

After he had the dishes back in the cupboard, he returned to the stable. The red, sticky substance was back. "What in the hell!" Greg normally didn't swear. Again, he cleaned it up and climbed the ladder to check the loft. Still, there was nothing unusual. He would keep this to himself; Lisa didn't need the added stress. Maybe later he would confide in Steve, Lisa's sister's husband.

When he got back in the house, Lisa was sound

asleep on the sofa in the parlor. Maggie was in a large chair in the corner quietly reading to one of her babies. He was aware she was partially reading the pictures, but that she knew many of the words. He started a fire in the fireplace and turned on some low romantic music—later he wondered if this was the best choice. He longed for Lisa's closeness.

Greg watched Maggie as she read her book. Her eyes were starting to close. It had been a long day, and she hadn't taken a nap. She was still dressed in the clothes she had worn for the day. Greg decided to wait until she fell asleep and then carry her upstairs and put her to bed, instead of waking her to get her jammies on. That would wake her up and wind her up again. He loved all Maggie's little stories, her smiles, and her giggles—but tonight he had other things on his mind. His thoughts went to the stable. The reappearance of the red substance was very much on his mind. It was such a puzzle. He first thought it had been dripping from the trap door. Now he wondered if it had come up from the floor.

After putting Maggie to bed and covering Lisa, he rummaged through some boxes, found the flashlight he was looking for, and headed out to the stable. As he opened the door into the back hallway, he stepped into something sticky. He shined the flashlight on it. This could not be. It appeared to be the same substance he had found earlier in the stable—a bit too eerie. The soles of his shoes were covered. Lisa must not see this. He opened the back servants' door and proceeded to walk across the lawn to the carriage house. There was a streak of light, somewhat like he had seen previously, which disappeared into the night. An uneasy feeling came over him. He quickly cleaned off his shoes, grabbed some more rags, and headed back to the house where he wiped up the sticky substance. He wet some paper towels in the kitchen and returned to finish cleaning the floor—fighting the urge to check the carriage house again.

A gentle kiss on the forehead and Lisa was awake. "What time is it?" she asked.

"10 o'clock."

"Oh, no, where did the evening go?" Lisa yawned.

"You were extremely tired, so I let you sleep. Maggie read until she fell asleep in the chair. I carried her up to bed. Let's go up to bed ourselves." He folded the throw and placed it on the arm of the sofa, then took Lisa's hand to help her off the sofa. Greg had to admit the bed felt awfully good. Lisa was soon asleep. He lay there trying to block out the bad events of the day, and then fell asleep picturing how the new furniture would look in his office.

*

The next morning, Greg was downstairs brewing coffee, when there was a knock at the back servants' entrance. He opened the door to see a man, possibly in his fifties, carrying an old, dented toolbox in one hand. His salt and pepper hair looked as if it hadn't been combed in days. He had at least a three-day whisker stubble and was shabbily dressed in jeans worn thin, with holes in the knees. His shirt was tattered, with buttons missing.

"Mornin'," he said with a smile. It was then when Greg noticed he had several front teeth missing. "I'm Hank Star. You called me about some remodelin'?"

"Yes, come in please. I'll show you what I have in

mind." Greg led him up the back stairway and down the hall, all the time thinking how he must not judge Hank for his appearance. For, he too, had buttons missing off a shirt. With this thought, he gave a muffled chuckle. He showed Hank what he wanted done with the room adjacent to the master bedroom. He could hear Lisa stirring, so he stopped to warn her that the carpenter had arrived—lest she run down to the shower half naked. He escorted her and went back to get Maggie. Maggie was awake and dressed, dressing her dollies. The two went downstairs to fix breakfast. Later, Lisa came down the back stairs. She would meet Hank in a while. This old house was too large to be meeting strange men, alone; especially a man looking like Greg had described him. She chuckled as she thought of his missing buttons, which Greg had mentioned. She doubted very much his buttons had suffered the same ill effects as Greg's had.

Once breakfast was over, Greg went back upstairs, where Hank was preparing to tear out the back wall of the bedroom closet. Greg hung a sheet to help keep the dust from filtering into the master bedroom. He was beginning to regret not remodeling this room before moving in. He felt it was going to be a dusty mess, besides being unsure of how trustworthy Hank was. He decided to go downstairs and make a phone call to Mr. Peterson who had recommended him. He explained his concerns to Mr. Peterson.

"Ole Hank? Naw, he wouldn't hurt a soul. He is a good person. He just doesn't happen to live in the world of fashion. He doesn't care how he dresses or what others think of the way he dresses. He has done odds and ends carpenter jobs in the area for years. Don't worry about Ole Hank. He will do a swell job for you, and he won't cause any trouble."

This was a big relief to Greg. Now he could relax; after all, he had two females to take care of. In fact, maybe it was a good idea to have another man around, after what he had seen yesterday. This blood-like substance was a real concern.

Greg looked in on the girls, as he headed out to the carriage house. They were in the sewing room checking to see if everything was where they wanted it. It looked to Greg as if they were still undecided about a few things. So was he.

Everything looked quite normal in the carriage house. If he hadn't known better, he would have thought the red substance had been a dream. He could find no trace of it, or any possible reason for it. He knew only that he was uncomfortable in this part of the carriage house.

Two

It was now June. The new master bath and walk-in closet have been completed. Hank has also finished Greg's office, and the furniture has arrived. Greg is now spending many hours in his office. This room has become his favorite hide-a-way. He loves the peacefulness of it; although at times he wishes it were a little closer to the sewing room where Lisa and Maggie spend much of their time. There have been no reoccurrence of the red, sticky substance. Greg has kept these incidents to himself, but he definitely has not forgotten them.

Lately, Lisa has been extremely tired. Greg was concerned she was overdoing with such a large house to take care of. She napped almost every afternoon and was still dragging by bedtime. She had her own thoughts on this, which she hadn't shared with Greg. He was unaware that she was nauseous at times. She had an appointment with her gynecologist, as she was sure she was in the early stages of pregnancy. She wanted to surprise Greg with the official word.

Lisa's appointment was with Dr. Rhonda Fontell, the obstetrician who delivered Maggie and had been her gynecologist since then. Lisa had always loved her and felt at ease with her. Dr. Fontell had two children of her own. Being female, she understood the concerns of a pregnant woman. Lisa hadn't told Greg she had an 11:00 AM appointment. She had led him to believe she was going for an early lunch, and some shopping with her close friend, Marta. She and Marta had been best friends since high school. They were a lot alike and both were interior decorators. Marta kept quite busy working from her home for some of the wealthiest people in town. She and Lisa met often for lunch and shopping. They had a special relationship. Lisa confided in Marta about most things.

While Lisa was in town, Maggie would help Greg with some late planting. It had been a wet spring, making it difficult to do much gardening earlier. Before the spring rains started, Greg managed to rototill the garden area, but he had been unable to do any planting. The potatoes were far beyond Good Friday planting. They would definitely be a late crop.

Lisa cleaned up the breakfast dishes and was on her way to Dr. Fontell's office at the physicians' office building, attached to Galena-Stauss Hospital. She felt fortunate there was a hospital in this small town. As she turned onto Summit Street, she could see the parking lot was full, as usual. Lisa had often felt the clinic needed more parking spaces. After all, many who visit the clinic are ill and don't feel like searching for ten minutes for a parking space. Maybe they needed valet parking. A car backed out of a parking stall, and Lisa was able to pull in before the car behind her was able to get to it. She felt guilty for taking the spot, but why should she? She had as much right to it as the other lady. Just the same, she could feel the disgust the lady in the other car was feeling toward her—the same disgust she had often felt when someone had taken a spot before she could get to it. It was getting close to eleven. Lisa hated being late for appointments; even though she knew once she got inside it would mean waiting for Dr. Fontell, as it was with most other doctors.

As usual, the waiting room was full. Many were flipping through magazines. Others were waiting impatiently, as they sat waiting for their names to be called. There were still many sitting in the waiting room when the nurse came to the door and called, "Lisa Carrington."

The other ladies must be waiting for another doctor, Lisa thought to herself.

After stepping off the scale, she was escorted to what she called a little room, where the nurse took her blood pressure and asked a few questions. When was her last period? Had she any spotting between periods, etc.? Lisa answered all the questions except the one about when her last period was. She had been so consumed with the move that she had forgotten to mark it on the calendar. The date had escaped her.

Lisa was handed a paper gown—one of those wonderful inventions. She was asked to remove all her clothes and put the paper gown on with the opening in the front. The so-called gown was more of a jacket. A paper sheet would serve as the bottom portion. Lisa felt this was degrading—one wrong move and a large rip could leave her exposed.

Dr. Fontell opened the door. "Hi, Lisa, what seems to be the problem?"

Lisa told her of her fatigue and nausea. Dr. Fontell then wanted to do a pelvic exam. Lisa scooted forward and Dr. Fontell placed Lisa's feet in the stirrups. She was glad she had a female doctor. This was embarrassing enough without the doctor being male.

When the exam was completed, Dr. Fontell helped her scoot back and sit up. "Lisa, I see no signs of pregnancy. Your uterus is normal size. Of course, you could be in a very early stage of pregnancy. I would like for you to go to the lab. They will draw blood for a serum pregnancy test. This will be more accurate than a urine test at this stage."

Lisa dressed and found her way to the lab, where two vials of blood were drawn. Her doctor would notify her when the results were in. She returned to the parking lot, giving someone else a place to park as she pulled away, in such deep thought that she vaguely noticed the car waiting to pull into her parking stall. She had hoped to be giving Greg the exciting news of a pregnancy today. This wouldn't discourage her, as Dr. Fontell had mentioned this could be an early stage of pregnancy. After all, she had been nauseous with Maggie quite early in that pregnancy.

As she drove into the driveway, she saw Greg and Maggie behind the house working in the garden. Maggie was dropping seed potatoes in the furrows Greg had made.

Greg came over to the car. "Short lunch date wasn't it?"

"We decided to skip shopping. Marta had something come up with a client at the last minute," Lisa fibbed. She hated not telling Greg the truth, but she must, in order to surprise him with the news later.

"Maybe you can get together again soon. I know how the two of you love to shop. Maggie and I went in for lunch a bit ago. I made us sandwiches and heated a can of tomato soup. Maggie is having such fun helping plant the garden—guess I'd better check and see how she's doing with the potatoes. We wouldn't want them all growing in one clump," he chuckled.

Lisa got out of the car and walked toward the servants' entrance, thinking how wonderful it would be to have a new little one in the house. Greg would be pleased, too—although she knew he had wanted to wait a while longer, until they were more settled and she was more rested. He had also hoped she could take on a few interior decorating jobs before she became too busy with a new little one.

Lisa made herself a salad and sat to relax a few minutes before changing clothes. She ate in the sewing room, so if Greg walked in he wouldn't see her eating. He would be curious as to why she was eating, when he thought she had just come from a lunch date. Looking at her mom's rocker in the sewing room made her think of when Maggie was a baby. Everything reminded her of babies these days. She was continuing to dream of a baby crying. It must be because of her desire to have another baby, she had decided. The dreams increased her desire. She was puzzled as to why the baby's cry sounded troubled. She hoped this didn't mean there would be something wrong with her baby. She would be glad when Dr. Fontell called confirming her pregnancy.

After lunch, Lisa went upstairs to change clothes, exhausted from her trip to the doctor. The bed looked inviting. She stretched across the queen-size canopy bed and was fast asleep within minutes.

She awoke with Greg's kiss on the lips. "Sleepy gal, again today, I see." Lisa stirred enough to return his kiss. "Amy and her mom came by and asked to take Maggie to the afternoon matinee. I thought it would be good for her to spend some time with Amy. She hasn't been with anyone her age for a few weeks. And you know how much she has wanted to see Shrek 2. I knew you would agree, so I let her go. I had her wash up and change into some clean clothes. She put on her purple shorts and the little lavender shirt. I called the shirt purple. She was quick to correct me that it's lavender! You girls are so particular about such things."

Lisa looked up at him and smiled. "Are you finished with your gardening for the day?"

"I could be if you would like me to be," he grinned.

"I was thinking maybe we could spend some quality time in the Jacuzzi while Maggie is away."

"Amazing how we think alike. First, I think it would be a good idea if I wash off in the shower," Greg answered.

Lisa agreed. She was dressed in only a half-slip, bra, and panties—all light green, a Martha Stewart green, as Greg called it. Greg cupped his hand inside her bra, exposing a breast. He lowered his lips to the nipple and began to suck, as he couldn't resist the temptation. He loved her breasts and knew this would get her going. It always did.

"Honey, if you ever want to make it to the Jacuzzi, you'd better quit that, or we will be making love right here on the bed, with you in your dirty clothes."

He gave her a peck on the lips, as he tucked her breast back inside her bra, and gave her well-filled bra cup a soft pat. He then disappeared into the new adjoining bath. Lisa arrived as he was stepping out of his sexy black briefs, which never failed to excite her. They fit just snugly enough to show the outline of his arousal, which she took in her hand. She so loved to feel his progression, which now already had a head start. He reached around her; his fingers feeling for her bra hooks. One by one he unfastened them allowing her bra to drop to the floor, exposing her amazing breasts. He slowly slid her half-slip down her legs, leaving only her bikini panties, which he eased off her sexy ass and down her shapely thighs. Her heart began racing as he spread her thighs. His fingers became playful.

Lisa then worried he would detect the lubricant Dr. Fontell used for the exam. "Greg honey, we need to get the Jacuzzi ready. Why don't you take your shower while I run the water?" She turned on the gold plated faucet and added a few drops of the gardenia-scented bath salts, which Greg had given her as a surprise the day the Jacuzzi was completed. He lit the floating candles surrounding the tub, turned on soft music, and closed the shutters on the window to block the outside light. The room was now a perfect romantic setting. The tub had finished filling by the time Greg stepped out of the shower. Lisa could see he was quite ready! She handed him some wine from the small refrigerator they had filled with wine and chilled glasses. He popped the cork and poured two glasses while she held them.

Days earlier, Lisa had replaced their usual wine with non-alcoholic wine, suspecting she might be pregnant. She gave Greg the excuse it would be less tiring since she was still adjusting to the added responsibilities of the new house. He took the filled glasses from her and sat them on the ledge alongside the Jacuzzi, then took her hand to help her in, admiring her beauty, as always. The warm bubbling water with the floral scent felt quite relaxing. Greg handed Lisa one of the glasses of wine and took the other for himself. They sipped their wine as they relaxed listening to "Let's Make Love" by Faith Hill and Tim McGraw. Greg leaned in and kissed Lisa, immediately causing her to respond. She was now feeling in a much more romantic mood than she had been in for weeks. The kiss went on and on. Lisa orgasmed. Greg could never understand how she did this. He began fondling her delicious breasts. As he sucked on her erect nipples, first one, then the other, her body arched toward him. He reached into the water, feeling, massaging, and exciting her even more. She knelt over top of him, lowering herself onto him. She loved the feeling. His size was more than she could have ever dreamed of. She began to rhythmically ride him, first slowly, then faster as pleasures mounted. Suddenly, she came down hard on him. Water splashed and ran out onto the floor. They hardly noticed.

Greg became more vocal. Lisa was close to being out of control. They loved it when they became this involved. They reached their peak at the same moment. Greg lifted her out of the water and carried her into the bedroom, where they lay cuddling until sleep came.

Later, as Lisa was preparing chicken and dumplings for supper, Maggie came bouncing into the kitchen, "Oh, goodie, first my favorite show and now one of my favorite suppers! I had the bestest time. Amy and I had a bunch of fun. Her mommy let us pick any treat we wanted. I had gummy worms. Amy had sweet tarts. We sat way down front so we could see good. Wowie, was Shrek ever big!"

Lisa laughed, knowing even the tiniest of characters would appear large from the front row. All through supper, Maggie continued to tell of her exciting afternoon, an afternoon that was wonderful for all.

Greg helped Lisa with the dishes, as he knew she

was exhausted. The nap had helped; that was until their romantic frolic. Lisa and Maggie both turned in early. Greg worked in his office until long after they fell asleep. Things were busy at work, and he was finding it necessary to bring work home at times. He was almost ready to quit for the night, when he heard the cries of a baby. This haunted him, as did the unanswered questions with the mysterious, red substance.

*

The next morning, as Lisa was tidying up the house, the phone rang. "Lisa, your test results are negative. You are not pregnant. I am so sorry. I know how much you hoped you were." Dr. Fontell continued to say, "I think you should see Dr. Harris to be on the safe side. I have made an appointment for you, for this Friday at 2:00. He had a cancellation, and I was able to get you in then. Try not to worry." Lisa thanked her and hung up the phone.

"Try not to worry. That's easy for her to say. This isn't normal for me to be so tired and nauseous. Maybe I'm anemic. Surely, Dr. Fontell checked for anemia."

The next two days were long ones. Lisa continued to keep this to herself, as she didn't want to worry Greg needlessly. Her sister, Lori, had agreed to watch Maggie. Lori assumed it was a regular checkup, nothing more. Lisa would tell Greg afterward, as Maggie would be sure to alert him to the fact Mommy had gone somewhere and left her with Lori.

Lisa got right in to see Dr. Harris. This must be her lucky day, she thought...well, not really, or she wouldn't be here. Dr. Harris was a young doctor, mid-thirties Lisa guessed. "Good afternoon, Lisa. Dr.

Fontell tells me you haven't been yourself. I'm sorry for your disappointment. She also passed that along to me." Lisa lay there in her paper gown, as he examined her. She wasn't as comfortable with Dr. Harris as she had been with Dr. Fontell. He poked and prodded and did a thorough exam, asking, "Lisa, how long have you had the tenderness in your abdomen?"

"It has been there awhile. We moved recently. I may have strained some muscles moving boxes about."

"That may very well be, but I also have noticed you are slightly jaundiced. I think we should run some tests. I want you to have lab work done. I feel we should do an ultrasound of your abdomen. They can draw blood at the lab here, before you leave today. Let me have my nurse call the hospital and set up the ultrasound."

Lisa's mind was in a fog as she dressed. The nurse came back into the room, after she finished dressing, to tell her to report to the hospital the following Wednesday at 9:00 AM.

She agreed, and then went to the lab. "Lisa Carrington...Lisa Carrington." Lisa knew from the stern tone of the lab tech's voice that this wasn't the first time she had called her name. She led her to a cubicle in the back, where she drew many vials of blood. Lisa felt this was a bit excessive.

As she left the parking lot, she almost pulled out in front of another car. Her mind was on what Dr. Harris had said. "Slightly jaundiced...an ultrasound." On the way to pick up Maggie, she was deep in thought. *Maybe he thinks I'm pregnant and something is wrong—something that some rest and vitamins will fix. That's it. I'm pregnant and it was too early to show up in the test Dr. Fontell ran,* Lisa kept trying to convince herself.

It was going to be difficult to explain all of this to Greg. Before, she had always been open with him. Would he understand her keeping this from him? She would soon find out.

Supper was over and the dishes were done. Maggie was starting to wind down from her afternoon with Lori. Lori and her husband, Steve, lived on a farm on the outskirts of town. They had many animals, which Maggie adored, her favorite being the baby lambs. She had fed one of them a bottle, as there were too many for the ewe to nurse. The baby kittens were also a highlight of the day. Lisa had joked with her sister saying they should open a petting zoo for all the young children to enjoy, since they had so many small animals, which children enjoyed. They even had a pig named Charlotte. The baby lamb Maggie bottle-fed was named Mary. Maggie had giggled at the supper table, saying the baby kittens needed some mittens.

Greg now knew, of course, that Lisa had gone to town and left Maggie with Lori. What he didn't know was that Lisa had been to the doctor. Lisa would tell him after Maggie was asleep for the night.

They settled in the parlor for the evening. Maggie curled up in a chair with a book and fell asleep quite early, exhausted from her day at the farm.

"Greg, honey," Lisa began. "I went to see Dr. Harris today."

"So, that's why you went into town and left Maggie at the farm."

"Yes, honey. Dr. Fontell wanted me to see him."

"So, when did you see Dr. Fontell?" Greg inquired.

"The first of the week, when I told you I went to lunch with Marta."

"And you didn't have lunch with Marta? Why did

you tell me you did, if you went to see the doctor?"
Greg appeared disturbed.

"I wanted to surprise you. I thought I was going to
have good news for you after I saw her. I thought I was
pregnant, because I've been so tired and nauseated
much of the time."

"Sweetie, you said you thought you were. You
aren't?"

"I'm not sure, honey. Dr. Fontell says I'm not. I
wonder if Dr. Harris thinks I am. I had a blood test
Tuesday for pregnancy. It came back negative. She
wanted me to see Dr. Harris for his opinion on my
nausea and fatigue."

"And... what did he say?"

"He wants me to have an ultrasound. I have
tenderness in my abdomen, and he thinks I look a little
jaundiced. He didn't say so, but I wonder, though, if he
may suspect I'm pregnant since he wants to do an
ultrasound."

"He thinks you're jaundiced?" Greg asked.

"That's what he said."

"I knew your coloring looked a little different. I
never gave it much thought. Now that you mention it,
maybe you are jaundiced."

"I think you are both seeing things." Lisa sounded
disgruntled. She was beginning to get a little disgusted
with all today's modern technology—all the messing
around for a simple pregnancy.

Greg could tell she was upset. He tried to comfort
her by agreeing with her—even though he didn't
entirely. It didn't seem to help much, and he couldn't
blame her. He felt Dr. Fontell would never have sent
her to Dr. Harris, unless something was terribly wrong.
Greg was quite concerned, although he didn't let on to

Lisa. She hadn't told him when the ultrasound would be. He chose not to upset her anymore by asking. He turned on the stereo, which already had her favorite Faith Hill CD in the player. He drew her close to him and laid her head on his lap, rubbing her arm in an attempt to comfort her. She lay quietly staring off into space. She seemed to be focused on a large picture of her and her mom, which was taken years earlier when Lisa was only a few years old. It was remarkable how much Lisa now looked like her mom did back then. It almost looked as if it was a picture of Lisa and Maggie, as there were strong resemblances of Lisa in Maggie; although there was enough of Greg in Maggie to recognize the child in the picture wasn't Maggie.

Greg wished he could help Lisa. She was terribly troubled, with reason. He knew to stay close and hold her. To initiate sex tonight would only upset her more. He himself wasn't in the mood, as he was concerned about Lisa. He was wondering what the doctors suspected. He hoped the ultrasound was scheduled soon. The not knowing was difficult. With the thought of Lisa having something seriously wrong, he drew her close—extremely close. He gently kissed her. He wished it were winter—the warmth of a fire in the fireplace was always a comfort in cold weather. The music had long since stopped playing. Neither wanted to move to put another CD in. Later, they went up the spiral staircase to bed. Lisa clung to Greg throughout the entire night. She invited him to shower with her that next morning. He washed her back, and she his. There was no personal touching; neither felt the desire. As they stepped out of the shower, Greg handed her a towel.

She looked at him solemnly as she murmured the

words, "Wednesday, 9:00 AM."

"Let me go with you, sweetie."

"I'd like that, honey."

They dressed and went downstairs. Breakfast was very simple today—bagels, juice and coffee. Maggie came bouncing in from the back stairway. She seemed to think the steep stairs were adventuresome in the early mornings. After dark, adventuresome turned to spookiness for her. Little did she know, her daddy felt the same way—especially since the incident with the blood-like substance.

Greg scooted his chair under the table. "You two ladies be good today. It's time for me to go earn my paycheck." He gave Maggie a peck on the cheek and then turned to Lisa, softly kissing her on the lips. As he turned to leave, he whispered, "Don't worry sweetie. It will be alright, you'll see."

If only Greg could take his own advice. He was terribly concerned, because Lisa was rarely ill.

The next five days went by slowly. As they drove to the hospital for the ultrasound, they exchanged very few words. Lisa's mind flashed back to the time she had an ultrasound when she was pregnant with Maggie. It was such a happy, exciting time, knowing she was pregnant with their first child. She and Greg had chosen not to learn the baby's sex, as it would add to the excitement. Lisa was clinging to the hope this ultrasound would confirm a pregnancy. She knew, in all reality, that she might be seriously ill. It was best to think positive thoughts until faced with the negative. Her mind jumped to the room she would make into a nursery and how she could decorate it. Maybe this time it would be more practical to learn the baby's sex, in order to decorate the room in a more appropriate theme. A boy would be nice this time; although she was sure Maggie would rather have a little sister. There would be seven years difference in their ages—too much age difference for them to have much in common. A boy would serve Maggie's needs just as well. She would love helping take care of him, as she loves caring for her dolls.

Greg's mind was on the possibility of Lisa being quite ill. Since Lisa mentioned Dr. Harris' concern that she was slightly jaundiced, Greg was noticing the jaundice was getting worse.

As they pulled into the hospital parking lot, Greg leaned over and kissed Lisa. "Sweetie, whatever it is, we will deal with it. At least now we will know." Greg meant well. His words were less than reassuring.

Lisa checked in. "Down the hall and to the left," directed a lady at the front desk.

They were led to a room in the X-ray department, where a technician was waiting to perform the procedure. The gel the tech spread on Lisa's abdomen was cool, just like she remembered it from before. The screen was turned so Lisa couldn't see it while the tech ran the instrument over her abdomen. Greg watched both the screen and the tech's eyes. Lisa watched the tech's eyes and the expression on Greg's face. No one spoke. Greg saw concern in the tech's eyes, which was immediately portrayed to Lisa through Greg. The screen hadn't really told Greg much, except that it didn't look like the ultrasound did when she was carrying Maggie. All he had to go by was how the tech looked, and her actions.

She turned the machine off and wiped the gel from Lisa's abdomen. "Your doctor will have the report in the next couple of days. Call his office in three days and he should be able to give you the results by then."

Lisa dressed and they were on their way. Now, what were they supposed to think? Lisa's hopes of a baby were diminishing. Negative thoughts began to creep in. No, she wouldn't let them! "Greg, honey, do you have time to go to the new furniture store with me?"

"I have all day if you'd like. Sure, sweetie, we can go to the furniture store. I've wanted to see what it's like. I've heard good things about it from my colleagues. I hear the prices are good, too. Let me call the office." As he sent the number on his cell phone, he knew he couldn't concentrate on work anyway. Lisa needed him. He needed her. When he finished talking to the office he called Lori's number. "Lori, hi, could you watch Maggie awhile longer? We have some shopping to do."

"Sure, Greg, Maggie is too wrapped up in the new baby lambs to leave for a while, anyway. Do I dare ask how the ultrasound went?"

"It's another waiting game…a few days anyway." Greg ended the conversation since he didn't want to draw Lisa's attention back to the ultrasound. She was doing so well.

Lisa failed to comment on him calling Lori. "We need to find a bedroom suite for the guest room. I think it's time to finish the upstairs. Now that we have the Jacuzzi room finished and your office is complete, we can begin on the guest room. Soon we can decorate the room next to Maggie's too. I need to think a little on that room. Maybe we should remove the old wallpaper and paint it a pastel color for now."

"If you like, we can go to the wallpaper store. We can take a few books home for you to decide on the paper for the guest room. I'm glad we went ahead and removed the paper in that room. It shouldn't take long to decorate it. The woodwork is in good shape," Greg said.

"For that bed, I want to use one of the quilts Mom made. I have one in mind to use. I will need to match the wallpaper to it."

They pulled into the furniture store, which wasn't far from the hospital. Not a word was spoken about the ultrasound.

The store impressed them both and they quickly found two bedroom suites they liked. They decided on one, which was well constructed and moderately priced, and also had a matching armoire and chair. Since the furniture had to be ordered, they should be able to finish decorating the room by the time it arrived.

As they were leaving the store, Lisa caught a glimpse of the baby furniture. This brought her back to the realities of the day. They drove on to the paint and wallpaper store. Lisa browsed through many books before she decided on several to take home. Greg kept busy returning books to their proper cubbyholes in the wall. He was leaving the choice up to Lisa, as she knew what would look best. His job would be to hang it— and of course to nod with approval over her choice.

Three

The following Friday afternoon, Lisa received a phone call from Dr. Harris. "Lisa, can you come to my office in the morning?"

Lisa found it difficult to say anything. She immediately became alarmed. "You want me to come there, tomorrow?"

"Yes, Lisa, if at all possible. The ultrasound showed something a little irregular. We need to discuss it."

Lisa agreed to be there at 9:00 AM. The words *something a little irregular*, stuck in her mind. *I'm pregnant and something is wrong with the baby, perhaps a tubular pregnancy.* This would mean she would lose the baby, and it would also account for Greg not seeing a baby on the screen. He had confided that much in her that night, in the hours following the ultrasound.

Greg was later than usual coming home from the office. With Maggie there, it was difficult to talk to him about Dr. Harris's phone call. Greg hadn't expected her to hear anything yet. He sensed she was bothered by something that evening and assumed the ultrasound was weighing heavily on her.

After Maggie was in bed for the night, Lisa invited

Greg into the Jacuzzi to relax. He knew this would be something other than a romantic adventure. The word relax would mean just that. Still, he dimmed the lights, lit some scented candles, and poured some non-alcoholic wine and placed it on the ledge. He then helped Lisa into the warm bubbling water. He sat close to her and put his arm around her, as music played low in the background.

"You feeling okay, doll?"

"Dr. Harris called late this afternoon. He wants to see me in the office in the morning. The ultrasound showed something a little irregular. Honey..."

"Shhh," he placed his finger on her lips. "Don't even speculate. We will listen to what he has to say in the morning before we jump to any conclusions." They sipped wine as they sat quietly in the warm bubbling water. Greg applied some bath gel to a washcloth and gently washed Lisa's unresponsive body. He, too, felt no sexual desires, only concern for what was ahead. He was now finding it too difficult to think positive. They had always felt so fortunate in life. That is, until Lisa lost her mom to colon cancer. Since then, the realities of life had become more apparent. As much as Lisa loved her mom and missed her, she still remained positive for the most part. Greg feared this was about to change.

Lisa was extremely tired. Greg turned the TV on as they got into bed, hoping she could get her mind on something else and fall asleep. He cradled her in his arms. Sleep was a long time coming.

The alarm went off at 6:00 AM, a short night indeed. Marta picked Maggie up to take her for breakfast. This was to be a real treat for Maggie. She loved Marta and rarely was given a chance to eat breakfast in a restaurant. Before Maggie had a chance to suggest they go to McDonald's, Marta described the delicious pancakes they served at a grown—up restaurant in town. She wasn't in the mood to dine in the play yard at McDonald's. Somehow, the musty smell of children's tennies didn't appeal to her this morning. Marta glorified the pancakes this restaurant served by saying they topped their waffles with whipped cream and strawberries. She was sure if Maggie requested the same for her pancakes, they would oblige her. This excited Maggie.

*

They arrived at the doctor's office shortly before 9:00 AM. They were the only ones in the waiting room. Lisa's name was called almost immediately. There was no weighing in, no paper gown, and no little room with an examining table. They were seated in Dr. Harris's private office. Both Lisa and Greg were extremely nervous. This wasn't the normal doctor appointment.

Dr. Harris entered the room dressed in his street clothes. He shook Greg's hand and gently reached out and squeezed Lisa's hand before seating himself behind his desk. "Lisa, there is reason for concern in your ultrasound." Lisa held her breath, waiting for the explanation.

Greg also was alarmed. He managed to ask, "What did the ultrasound show?"

"The ultrasound was inconclusive. I want Lisa to be admitted to the University of Iowa Hospital in Iowa City, for further testing. We are small here. The University Hospital is a much better facility equipped to handle cases as these—much better than we can. It is important you have the best doctors, Lisa. There at the University Hospital, they will have a team of doctors to see you."

"Are you sure this is necessary?" Lisa asked.

"I feel it would be best to get to the bottom of this as quickly as possible, so we can deal with whatever the problem is."

Greg wanted to ask questions. He kept them to himself, so as not to alarm Lisa any more than she already was.

"I have called the University Hospital and made arrangements for you to be admitted Monday morning," Dr. Harris explained.

Lisa nodded. She could find no words.

Greg shook Dr. Harris's hand and thanked him. He then called Marta and asked if she could keep Maggie until early afternoon. He felt they needed time alone before Maggie arrived home. The drive home was extremely quiet. Many things were going through Greg's mind. The word cancer stuck in his mind—and in his gut.

Lisa was extremely quiet. She knew this wasn't good news. The baby she so hoped for was now dead, in her mind. She was adjusting to this besides trying to cope with the words reason for concern, inconclusive, Iowa City Hospital, team of doctors. It was too much to handle. Where was her positive outlook?

Greg wanted to help her. He was feeling so low himself that it was difficult to help her. Finally, he found the words. "Lisa, sweetie, this is tough. We both feel it. We will get through this together, whatever it is. Is there anything we can do this morning to help you?"

"Honey, this may sound like a poor idea to you, but…I want to visit Mom and take some flowers to her."

"Sweetie, this might be the best thing for you. I know how close you and your mom were. You shared everything. Your need to be with her now is understandable."

On the way to the cemetery, they stopped at the florist shop. The florist made up an assorted bouquet in a heavy ceramic vase. Even though Lisa knew the flowers wouldn't last long out in the weather, she wanted her mom to have them. When they arrived at the grave, Lisa placed the flowers at the headstone and knelt down beside the grave. Greg stepped back a few feet so she could be alone with her mom—silly, as it might seem. "Mom, I'm scared...very scared. The doctor wants me to go to the University Hospital in Iowa City. Something is seriously wrong. I feel it. Pray for me, Mom. Help me to overcome this fear and accept whatever it is. Lead the way for me, as I feel I will be with you soon. Pray for Maggie. Please help her. And Mom...Greg will need your help, too."

Lisa rose to her feet, with a calm Greg hadn't expected. "Let's go get Maggie. She loves to help remove wallpaper."

"You want to remove the wallpaper in that last room today?"

"Sure, what better time?"

"As a matter of fact, you are right. There is no time like the present. Let's stop at the paint store and see if we can rent the steamer." Greg said.

Maggie was excited at the thought of helping remove wallpaper. "Goodie," she exclaimed, "I am so totally sick of that stupid old wallpaper. Why did those people ever want such ugly flowers anyway?"

Lisa almost chuckled hearing her say she was

totally sick of the wallpaper. They picked up the steamer and headed home. Two blocks from home, a black cat ran in front of the car. *Oh, my God,* Greg thought, *We do not need this today!* He was glad Lisa had turned her head to say something to Maggie. She never saw the cat.

"Anyone for Sub sandwiches for lunch?" Greg asked.

"Hooray!" exclaimed Maggie.

"Sweetie, what do you think? I could run in and get them to take home to eat."

"Sounds great to me," Lisa answered.

"This way you won't have to fix any lunch and we can get started on the paper stripping," Greg suggested.

He knew before he asked that Maggie would order the meatball sandwich, and he was reasonably sure Lisa would order the grilled chicken. He preferred the steak sandwich himself. He grabbed some of their delicious M&M chocolate chip cookies. Maggie had forgotten to request them; he knew she would be upset if he didn't get one for her.

Maggie had fun scooping up the old paper, as it fell on the floor. Greg had carried a large garbage can upstairs to the room and lined it with a plastic garbage bag, making it easier to fill than if they had to hold a bag open. After stripping two walls, Greg and Lisa decided that was enough for the day. It was getting late. While Greg and Maggie finished cleaning up, Lisa ordered pizza. They settled in for the night with pizza and TV in the parlor.

Lisa was exhausted. It had certainly been a full day. Her mind was definitely not on the HBO movie Spiderman. Anyway, they had seen it at the theatre when it first came out. Maggie was requesting to see

Spiderman 2. Lisa was thankful they had kept busy; although it was evident her physical strength was much less than normal. Now, she realized there was more to it than the stress from the move and the upkeep of a larger house. She knew she was gravely ill, just as if she already had a diagnosis. She wasn't sure how she knew, she just knew.

The next morning they all went to church. Lisa prayed for guidance. Greg prayed Lisa would be okay—even though he had a gut feeling she wouldn't be. Maggie told God how happy she was and how much she loved Mommy, Daddy, Marta, Aunt Lori, Uncle Steve, and all the little animals.

After church, Greg continued stripping wallpaper. He stripped, and Maggie gathered up armloads putting it into the garbage can. Lisa quietly packed a few things she felt she would need at the hospital. She called Lori and asked her to watch Maggie—this time maybe for a few days, as Greg would be staying in Iowa City. Maggie would love a vacation at Aunt Lori's. Lisa packed a suitcase for Maggie. Ordinarily, Lisa would have had Maggie help pack. Today she wasn't up to all Maggie's chatter and questions. They would tell her later.

*

The drive to the University Hospital in Iowa City seemed much longer than two hours. Neither Lisa nor Greg had much to say. They were both extremely worried. Maggie had been told only that they were taking a little trip. She didn't like to travel and gladly stayed behind with Aunt Lori.

The hospital was very large compared to Galena

Stauss—so many buildings. After all, this was a large university. Admittance went smoothly, as most of the admittance information had been taken care of in advance. Lisa was shown her room, and within an hour she was settled in—as much as a new patient awaiting a diagnosis could be. A short time later, five doctors entered her room asking questions while examining her. Yes, her abdomen was still tender, even more so than it had been when examined by Dr. Harris. They explained they would be doing a series of tests in the next few days, tests that should bring about a diagnosis. The first tests would include an MRI, blood tests, and chest x-rays. The MRI was scheduled for early afternoon. Possibly after these tests results were in they would follow up with other tests, depending on what these first tests showed. Lisa and Greg were given little explanation as to what they expected to see in an MRI, except that a clearer picture of what was causing the tenderness in her abdomen was needed.

The results of the MRI were in by late afternoon. An ERCP was scheduled for the next morning. A flexible tube would be put down Lisa's throat, through her stomach, and into her small intestine. Then, dye would be injected into the duct of her pancreas, so the area could be seen more clearly on an x-ray. A fine needle would be inserted into her pancreas to take out cells to biopsy. By now, Lisa and Greg were extremely worried, too many tests and too few explanations. A pancreas biopsy was nothing to take lightly.

Greg had planned to find a motel room until the nurses told him he was welcome to sleep on a cot in Lisa's room. Since he didn't wish to leave her at a time like this, he agreed to the cot. Neither got much sleep. Lisa was taken to a procedure room at eight the next morning and the test was performed. When the results were in, the doctor group came in her room to explain what they had found.

"We have found cancer cells in your pancreas, Lisa. This is what is causing your abdomen to be so tender," explained a Dr. Stevens. "We are sorry to have to tell you this. We will need further tests to determine the extent of the cancer and what treatment will be necessary. The sooner we determine this, the quicker we can start treatment. We are scheduling a PTC for tomorrow morning. During this test, a thin needle will be put into your liver through your right side. Dye will be injected into the bile ducts in the liver, so blockages can be seen on X-rays."

Lisa and Greg appeared to be in shock. Now there was too much information, too fast. The doctors left the room. Greg sat on the bed beside Lisa and soon was lying beside her, with his arms around her. Neither spoke. What was there to say?

Morning came after a restless night. The nurses said nothing about Greg being in Lisa's bed.

The dye was injected into the bile ducts and the X-rays were taken. The doctors delivered the results late that afternoon. Yes, there were blockages in the liver. Surgery was recommended to relieve the blockages and to determine if there was cancer in the liver and other surrounding organs.

Dr. Stevens was quite straightforward with his words. "This surgery is very necessary, as we know the pancreas has malignancies, and possibly the liver, stomach or spleen. There is no way left, other than surgery, to determine just how far this cancer has spread." The doctors left the room after explaining a decision should be made soon.

Lisa wanted to leave the hospital. Greg agreed they needed time away from the hospital. They checked into a nearby hotel for the night. They lay in each other's arms, continuing to say very little.

Around midnight, Lisa whispered to Greg, "I need to get some fresh air. Let's go for a drive."

"Sweetie, if that is what you want, that is what we will do."

They drove for quite some time. They found a small park and sat watching the stars. Each was remembering how they often did this in their high school years. They returned to the hotel more relaxed, and finally fell asleep in each other's arms. They still hadn't discussed what the doctors had told them—they each knew the surgery was necessary.

By late morning, they returned to the hospital. Dr. Stevens was paged. They were led to a conference room, where Dr. Stevens appeared a few minutes later. Lisa told him her decision was to have the surgery as soon as possible. He had already scheduled the surgery, feeling the importance to move swiftly. Lisa was admitted to have the surgery the following day. Once she had settled in, Greg took her to the hospital chapel, where they knelt and prayed. Lisa prayed for strength to accept whatever would be found. Greg silently wept as he prayed, for he was terribly afraid of what they would learn the next day.

The night passed slowly, as neither slept much. Lisa was taken into surgery at 7:00 AM and was in recovery by 9:00 AM. Dr. Stevens appeared in the surgical waiting room where Greg was blankly staring at Newsweek magazine. "Mr. Carrington... " Greg looked up. Dr. Stevens was so somber that Greg knew immediately the news was bad. "We were able to repair the blockages in your wife's liver. This should make her more comfortable with less tenderness in her abdomen. The cancer is not only in her pancreas; it is also in her liver, as we suspected. We did a frozen section biopsy on her stomach and spleen. I am sorry to tell you, there are cancer cells in both her stomach and spleen..."

Greg asked no questions. Dr. Stevens' words seemed to trail off, until they faded totally. Greg heard nothing of his last words. Dr. Stevens turned and left the room. Greg was in shock. A nurse appeared and led him to Lisa's room, where she sat with him until he became more responsive. She left the room telling him Lisa would be in recovery for another hour or so and then would be brought back up to her room.

Greg felt as if he had been struck by lightning. What would he say to Lisa? How could he tell her the gruesome outcome of the surgery? He needed answers himself. He thought back to how the doctor's words had faded out. He wondered what he hadn't heard. Regardless, he knew Lisa didn't have a chance. His precious, precious, sweetheart—Lisa was his life. How could he go on if she was taken from him?

Lisa was wheeled in on a gurney, looking quite pale, drowsy, but awake.

Greg kissed her on the forehead, "How ya doin', sweetie?" She only nodded and closed her eyes. Greg sat by her side. Even now, her beauty was showing through. She was the most beautiful person he had ever known—inside and out. Her inner beauty was even more remarkable. She was a wonderful loving mom to Maggie and the most passionate loving wife a man could ever ask for. *How could God do this to her? How could he do this to me? And Maggie? Life sucks!*

Lisa was too groggy to understand anything Greg

could say to her at this point. He was thankful for this, as the words to tell her what they had found seemed to be nonexistent at this time. How would he ever find the words?

She slept for some time, coming to occasionally long enough to know Greg was at her side. Then she would fall back asleep. When she finally awoke, Greg was still searching for the words to tell her.

Their eyes connected and Lisa whispered, "Honey, you don't need to say anything. I know it's bad. I have felt this since the day Dr. Harris referred me here to this hospital. Your eyes now tell me I was right." She drifted off to sleep.

Greg was relieved he was spared telling her. He only wished there was some way he could help her.

He took the elevator down to the first floor to the chapel, where he sat silently—still in shock. In a few short minutes his life had changed. The gal he had made his life, and the one he loved so dearly, would soon leave him. This couldn't be. Lisa was meant to be with him forever. Forever...how long is forever? He dwelled on this for some time. The answer came to him. Everyone's forever is of a different length, a different time. Lisa's forever was to be soon. He began to pray. He prayed Lisa wouldn't have to suffer a horrible cancer death. He prayed she could be spared the pain, as her mom had been, with her colon cancer. Hers was a rapid death. Hospice had gone to the house and set up a hospital bed in her living room. She died that night.

He prayed Lisa would suffer very little. He prayed she would find the strength to cope with whatever was ahead. Then, he thought of how the doctor's words had trailed off. Had he missed something? Was there hope for her?

When Greg arrived back at Lisa's room, the doctor group was there. They proceeded to explain what they had found. "Lisa, your cancer has spread to many of your organs—the stomach, spleen, and liver all show signs of malignancies. There are three possible alternatives for treatment:

1.Insert radioisotopes through thin plastic tubes into the area where the cells are found.

2. Chemotherapy

3. Do nothing

We want you to understand neither radiation nor chemotherapy will be a cure; although, they could slow down the progression and possibly help with the pain."

Greg thanked them. They expressed their regrets and left the room. Greg scooted his chair closer to Lisa. He wanted to lie beside her. He was afraid he would jar her and cause her more pain. The silence was obvious. They needed time to absorb what the doctors had said. At least, Greg felt they did.

"Do nothing," Lisa quietly whispered.

"Sweetie, take your time to decide. You needn't give them your decision so soon."

"I have seen the suffering others have experienced with both chemo and radiation. If there could be a chance to be cured, sure I would want treatment. Without a cure, either would only make my valuable days full of suffering. I want to spend my time with you and Maggie, with life as normal as possible. To be going back and forth to doctors and hospitals, would fill my days with appointments and running, leaving little time for you and Maggie—not to mention how sick the treatment would make me feel."

Three days later, Greg drove Lisa home. Maggie

was so excited to have her mommy back home again. She had yet to be told. Lisa felt the time would come soon enough. For now, she wanted their life to be as normal as possible. She first needed to heal from the surgery. She was still quite sore, as was to be expected. Greg had taken some time off to be home with Lisa. She was surprisingly in good spirits. Greg felt she must be in the stage of denial. It had all come about so suddenly, or so it seemed.

*

Within a few weeks, Lisa was feeling much better. She continued to tire easily, although she was able to function quite well. They had always spent most of their time together as a family. Now it had much more meaning than before. They made every minute of every day count. Lisa and Greg took Maggie to Brookfield Zoo in Chicago. She enjoyed seeing all the animals. There were so many more animals than at Aunt Lori's. She couldn't decide which she liked best—the bears, the monkeys, or the big elephants. She jabbered all the way home about what a special day it had been. She was wound up. She almost made it all the way home before falling asleep. Greg carried her into the house with her new stuffed monkey clenched in her hand, close to her chest, and laid her on the sofa in the parlor. He then went back to help Lisa. The day had been quite wearing on her. Many times she and Greg sat on a bench to rest, while they watched Maggie giggle over the animals. She would mimic first one animal and then another. Yes, it had been a most enjoyable day— "The mostest fun", as Maggie had described it.

After tucking Maggie into bed for the night, Greg

filled the Jacuzzi. He helped Lisa undress and step into the tub. As he placed his clothes on the chair, he noticed Lisa was watching him. She made no effort to reach out for him. Their time together was relaxing, although not the sexual, sensual time it had been before the diagnosis. Neither felt much like sex. They were hurting. It was difficult to think of sex, when they had so many other thoughts running through their heads. Lisa was concerned about how Greg and Maggie would manage without her. Greg was mostly concerned about how Lisa was feeling. He found it difficult to put what was ahead, out of his mind. On the other hand, it was almost difficult to believe Lisa was gravely ill, and that her time with them would soon be cut short.

Lisa spent as much time with Maggie as she could during her summer vacation from school. She read to her even more than usual, although she had always spent a lot of time reading to her. They played children's card games and board games. They went shopping for fabric. Lisa made several little outfits for Maggie. She crocheted little doll blankets for her dollies.

Lisa had taught her to pray when she was less than two years old. They prayed more now.

One night in her evening prayers, Lisa was surprised when Maggie said, "And Jesus, one more thing, one very important thing—please help my mommy. She is very sick. Please help her to not hurt. She is a good mommy. She shouldn't hurt. And Jesus, please…be her friend, her special friend, when she comes to live with you."

Lisa was shocked. She and Greg were still searching for the right time to tell Maggie. Somehow, she already knew. Maggie climbed into bed. Lisa pulled the covers up under her chin, "Maggie, honey, who told you Mommy is going to live with Jesus?"

"Grandma did," Maggie whispered, as she closed her eyes.

Lisa was amazed at how quickly Maggie was asleep. Did she really understand her mommy was dying?

Lisa looked up, as if to look up to heaven, "Thank-you, Mom. Thank-you for sparing me having to tell Maggie."

Greg came upstairs as Lisa was leaving Maggie's room.

"Hon, how about if we relax in the bedroom tonight? We can listen to music, read, or talk, whatever you would like," he suggested.

"That sounds nice, honey. Some music would be great. How about 'Let's Make Love'?"

"Are you asking for the Faith Hill song, or to make love?" Greg asked.

"I was thinking of both," Lisa smiled. Greg gave her that sexy smile of his and helped her into a comfortable cotton nightie he had purchased for her after she became so thin. She didn't feel so much like dressing beautifully or sexy anymore. She catered toward being comfortable. Greg still thought she was beautiful, even though she was a little thin. Of course, he still felt she was sexy. She was just too tired and weak to act sexy. Greg slipped on a pair of sleep shorts, which he had worn very little until recently. He put on the Breathe CD, one of Faith Hill's, and slipped into bed beside Lisa, put his arm around her, and cuddled her for a few minutes.

"Are you sure you are up to this, sweetie?" he whispered.

"I think it will be okay if we don't get too rough."

"Rough, who gets rough?" Greg winked. He

slipped her nightie up and lovingly entered her. Ever so gently, he penetrated her with rhythmic motions. Much to his surprise she was beginning to respond. She began to moan in soft whispers, as she thrust gently toward him. He kissed her breasts, remembering how turned on she used to get as he played with them. Did he dare now, or would it wear her out too much?

Lisa must have known what he was thinking, "Sweetie, play with them."

Greg began gently fondling her sensitive breasts. Her response wasn't the usual, but the important thing was that they had again shared their intimate love. They lay closely, listening to Faith Hill, until Lisa fell asleep, obviously quite tired from making love. Greg lay there looking at her, thinking, praying for a miracle; although he knew it would take one huge miracle to save her.

The next morning, as they were getting dressed to go downstairs, Lisa looked at Greg, and said, "Honey, Maggie knows."

"How do you know that?"

"She asked Jesus in her prayers last night to be my special friend, when I come to live with him. I asked her who told her this. She said, 'Grandma did.'"

Greg held her tightly. He couldn't bear the thought of her leaving—dying. He went in to the office later that morning. It was getting extremely difficult to go to work and leave her, as he wanted to spend every minute with her.

After Greg left, Lisa and Maggie went to the farm. Steve took Maggie out to the farmyard to give Lisa and Lori a chance to talk. Lisa had, of course, told Lori of her cancer. She hadn't been ready to talk much in detail.

Once they were alone, Lisa opened up to Lori. "Lori, I know my days are short. My body is weaker, and I have little strength now to do the things I want to do. I want to stay home as long as possible, although I don't want Maggie to see me suffer. I know cancer deaths, many times, are much less than a pretty sight. Maggie is so young. I want to spare her the gruesomeness of death. I want her to remember me, as I am now, not some pitiful suffering person. My death will be difficult enough for her. Please help her all you can. She loves being here with you and Steve and all your animals.

And Greg, my wonderful, wonderful, loving husband—he is my strength, my love. To have to leave him hurts deeply. So few are fortunate to find a love like ours. He is more than the typical male…much more. He is such a sensitive, caring, passionate man. He seems to know my every need before I do and sees that everything I need and desire is within my reach. Leaving him will be the hardest thing I have ever had to do. He is my life. I know life is eternal, but how can I live on without him by my side?

I am very concerned about him. He will grieve terribly…I know him. I want him to go on with his life. Marta has always envied me for having found Greg. My hope is the two of them can be together after I pass on. Maggie loves Marta—always has. Marta is so much like me. I know, in time, Greg could learn to love her. Please Lori, do what you can to get them to spend time together. I plan to write letters to both Greg and Maggie. I will give Maggie's to Greg to give to her when she gets older. I will place Greg's in my jewelry box. Will you see that he finds it?"

Lori had sat quietly listening to Lisa, wiping back tears as Lisa spoke. It was difficult to believe this was happening. Lisa would die, and probably soon. "Of course, I will see to it he finds the letter. You know I will." She began to sob. Lisa reached out to her. They held each other, as they cried.

Four

As the days passed, Lisa became increasingly weaker. She spent much of her time resting. Maggie was now in school. Lisa missed Maggie being by her side; although it was best, as she could rest more during the day and conserve what little strength she had for evenings when Greg and Maggie were both home. Most evenings were spent quietly together. They played board games with Maggie, watched movies, and basically just enjoyed being together. Maggie was in bed early on school nights, giving Lisa and Greg precious alone time, now more precious than ever. There was more closeness these days than sex, as it was tiring for Lisa. They lived each day for what it was, trying not to look ahead, although when each was alone, their thoughts most often went to the future—a future they no longer would have together. Who would have ever thought their time together would be so short? They were grateful for little Maggie. She brought such joy. Lisa couldn't bear the thought of leaving her, such a precious and loving child. To leave her without a mommy at such a young age was not fair to her, nor was it fair for Lisa to have so few short years with her. She envied Greg for being able to stay with Maggie.

Oh, how Maggie would need him.

It was now time to write good-bye letters to Maggie and Greg. Time was slipping away, and Lisa was aware of this. She sat at her desk, with her pen in hand, staring at her stationery with tiny pink roses—Maggie's favorite. It was difficult to know what to write. She thought for some time, before putting her pen to the paper. She asked herself, "What would Maggie need most to hear at age twelve? What did she want most to say to Maggie?" Finally, she began to write.

Maggie honey,

Mommy loves you. I didn't want to leave you. God wanted me with him. Sometimes choices aren't ours to make. By now, you are a young lady. I have missed being with you for so many special occasions—birthdays, Christmases, and other holidays. I was so blessed to have you as my little girl for the time that I did. The day you were born was the best day of my life. You were such a beautiful little baby. I knew as soon as the doctor laid you in my arms that you were a very special little girl. Daddy and I loved you so much, even before you were born. Someday, you will know what I mean, when you have your own children. I have loved you more each day, as I have learned to know your cute little ways. You have been such a loving child. No mommy could have asked for a sweeter little girl. We had hoped to give you a brother or sister, but God had other plans. We are not told what his plans are. We must trust that he has a reason for the things that seem unfair to us. Maybe, as you read this, I have already learned his reason for me having to leave you. My faith tells me that I will be able to watch you grow from above, as there are holes in the floor of heaven—holes where I can still share the pleasure of you. I asked Daddy to give you this letter on your twelfth birthday. Honey, know that I am watching you, as you read this— watching you and loving you. You will soon be a teenager, a beautiful teenager, I am sure. I am hoping that Daddy has found a new mommy for you by now, as little girls should not grow up without mommies. Sure, I will always be your mommy, but it is wonderful to be special enough to have two mommies. You have grown up so quickly. Soon, if not now, you will be getting interested in boys. Yes, you will! I hope you will be fortunate enough to find a guy as special as your dad. Your dad always had a way of making me feel loved and very special. These are very important qualities in a man. Without these, a marriage will be missing something special. Your heart will guide you.

Take good care of your dad. He will always be special to me, as our love was very special.

Know that I will love you for all eternity, and someday we will be together again.

Much Love,
Mommy

Lisa, her eyes wet with tears, folded the letter and put it in a pink envelope with Maggie's name on it and sealed it. This had been an extremely difficult letter to write. Now, it was time to write her good-bye to Greg. "How can I ever tell him good-bye? How can I leave him? He is my life. My precious, precious Greg!" She walked over to the window and looked down at the side yard. The flower garden Greg had planted for her was still in full bloom. The flowers were so beautiful now—the most beautiful they had been all summer. The first frost would come soon. It seemed such a shame that just as the flowers reached their prime beauty they would have to die—just as she had to die, at such a prime time in her life.

Lisa again sat at her desk, wiping tears away. Life was so unfair. "Why, God, why?" she asked. "Why would you ask me to leave such a wonderful life? Why would you bless me with such a wonderful loving husband and equally wonderful little girl, only to make me leave them?" She knew of so many unhappy people, so many unhappy marriages, and so many women with husbands that didn't love them as Greg loved her. It made no sense to her why she had to leave. Her faith told her she was not to question God. How could she not, at a time like this? She had tried to be strong for Greg. She also knew that Greg was not as strong as he wanted her to believe. In actuality, he was crumbling inside. He had made her and Maggie his whole life. She knew better than anyone how his happiness depended on them.

She began to write…

My dearest, darling Greg,

If you are reading this, I have passed on to a more beautiful place—if there can really be a place more beautiful than my life with you and Maggie. I have asked Lori to be sure you find this letter soon after my death…

When she finished the letter, she enclosed it in another pink envelope with the scent of her favorite perfume and tucked it away in a drawer in her jewelry box, where Greg would find it.

Being quite tired, she stretched out on the bed and covered up with an intricately designed, ivory afghan crocheted for her by her mom. Of the many her mom had made for her, this had always been her favorite.

*

Greg left work early, as something told him he must go

home. He could feel Lisa's presence, as if she was there with him. He felt she must have needed him. As he approached the house, a strange feeling came over him. He ran into the house and up the spiral staircase. There she lay on their bed, covered with the afghan, sleeping ever so peacefully. He was unable to wake her. Feeling a sense of panic, he called 911.

The paramedics arrived in a few short minutes. After examining Lisa, one of the men turned to Greg, and solemnly said, "Mr. Carrington, I'm sorry... she's gone." Greg couldn't believe what he was hearing. He knew she had been getting weaker. It hadn't entered his mind that she could be so near death. How could she have died already...and alone? He should have been with her.

The rest of the day was a blur for Greg. He remained in a state of disbelief. His Lisa could not be gone.

The next morning, Greg and Lori went to the funeral home to make the arrangements. A nicely groomed, middle-aged man, wearing a black suit, greeted them and escorted them to the back of the room, toward the stairs. All this time, Greg was wondering where Lisa was. He was finding it difficult to believe his Lisa was lying in a room somewhere in that funeral home...dead. Was she behind the closed door he just walked past? Or, was she upstairs? Was she being embalmed at that very moment? He was numb, but yet hurting deeply. He wasn't sure how it was possible to feel both at the same time. Somehow...he did.

They were taken up to the second floor, to the room where the caskets were displayed. Seeing all the caskets lined up, knowing he had to choose one for his precious Lisa was overwhelming, and almost more than he could handle. He choked back tears, as he slowly walked around looking at each one. He wanted something special. He came to one, like no other he had ever seen. He knew immediately this was the one he wanted. It was an elegant ivory with gold hardware. The inside was off white, with delicate embroidery of shades of pinks and purples on the inside of the lid—the embroidered letters spelled out "Our precious love". Tears now streamed down his face. Lori choked back tears, wanting to run from the funeral home to escape this nightmare. Instead, she found strength and comforted Greg. Together, they chose a vault, and were then taken downstairs to make the final arrangements. Greg was glad Lori was there with him. She was hurting as much as he was. Somehow, they were able to give each other support.

One last stop was to the florist shop. Greg chose a large casket spray of pink rose buds, with a plum colored ribbon, with gold lettering spelling, *Your Loving Husband*. For Maggie, he chose a small casket pillow with *Mommy* embroidered in pink, with one single pink rose bud attached. Lori and Marta had already been there and placed their orders. Lori and Steve asked for a ceramic vase of large pink lilies, purple larkspur, white roses, and miniature purple carnations with a sage green ribbon, with *Sister* in gold lettering. Marta had ordered a huge basket of shades of pink silk roses and tulips, and white baby's breath, with a purple ribbon and silver lettering saying, *Best Friend*.

When Greg and Lori got back to the house, they went to the walk-in closet to choose Lisa's clothes. There, hanging in front of everything, was the designer blend, dark plum suit and pink satin blouse Lisa had bought last spring, when she and Marta went shopping after a lunch date. A plastic bag hung from the same hanger, containing a light pink slip, bra, and panties, which Greg had given her for Valentine's Day.

"Oh, my God!" exclaimed Greg.

He had gotten a pair of slacks from her rack for her just that morning, before leaving for work. These clothes weren't hanging there then. He knew that, somehow, she knew she would die that day. He began to sob. "Why didn't I stay home with her? How could I not have known?"

Steve had taken Maggie out to the farm. She had been told her mommy had gone to heaven. She cried at first, and then soon acted if nothing was wrong. Greg wondered if she understood. She was so young, too young to lose her mommy.

Before leaving for the funeral home with Lisa's clothes, Lori told Greg where to find the letter. In Lisa's jewelry box, he found two pink envelopes, one addressed to Greg, *my darling* and the other to *Maggie*. His was left unsealed. He opened it and began to read.

My dearest, darling Greg,

If you are reading this, I have passed on to a more beautiful place—if there can really be a place more beautiful than my life with you and Maggie. I have asked Lori to be sure you find this letter soon after my death. Oh, Greg honey, what can I say? I wanted so much to stay with you. You are so precious. Never could I have found a man more wonderful, more loving, or sexier than you. I knew from the moment I met you that you were my love, the man I must spend the rest of my life with. Little did I know that it would be such a short life. God better have a darn good reason for this! We must accept this, and you must go on. You must not grieve for long, honey. Life is too short to spend it in grief. Make Maggie's days happy ones. She has lost her mommy; don't let her lose her daddy to grief. God will be sure to help you. I will help you all I can. Surely, God will give me that much.

In time, you must find someone else to share your life with—a new mommy for Maggie. Yes, honey, I want you to marry again. I know right now this may seem impossible. You will know when the time is right. Please, don't hesitate on my account. There is no set time that you must be alone before you begin to see another. Who cares what people think! I know you love me and will never forget me. This doesn't mean you can't learn to love another. This is what I want for you. You are too young to spend the rest of your life alone—too young and too sexy!

Maggie is too young to understand the totality of all this. Please see that she gets her letter on her twelfth birthday, when she will be more able to understand. Honey...give her a big kiss for me. I will miss you both, terribly. You know I believe in eternal life. I also believe I will be there with you, helping you with Maggie, helping you to go on, and to move on.

I love you more than I ever thought it was possible to love any man. You have given me the best. I never lacked for anything—especially love. Good-bye my darling.

Much, Much love,
Lisa

After reading this, Greg fell to the floor sobbing. "Oh, Lisa...you can't be gone!" He lay on the floor continuing to sob—wanting to go with Lisa. He couldn't bear the thought of going on without her. She was his life and had been since high school. How could this have happened, he wondered? Why did it happen? Two people so much in love should never be separated.

Then, he thought of Maggie; sweet little Maggie

would need him now, more than ever before. He got up off the floor and lay on the bed where Lisa had died. Suddenly, he felt overwhelming warmth and closeness to Lisa. He was exhausted and soon fell asleep.

In his sleep, he heard Lisa saying, "Greg, you have to be strong. I know this is difficult for you, but you must be strong for Maggie. I love you. I am fine. Please, don't worry about me. Take care of sweet, little Maggie." With this he awoke.

"What just happened? Did I dream Lisa was talking to me? It seemed so real." It was difficult for him to shake this dream, as it seemed so much like Lisa was there talking to him. He looked at the clock for the first time in hours.

Maggie would be home soon. Marta had offered to watch Maggie for the day, as they didn't feel she should be in school today, even though she appeared to be okay. Greg still wondered if she understood Mommy was not coming back.

So many people were being so good to help out. Many people loved Lisa. What was there not to love about Lisa? She was certainly a special person—one who loved everyone.

The front door opened, and in came Maggie and Marta. Maggie ran up to Greg and said, "I love you Daddy!" and gave him a big hug. Seemingly happy, she immediately ran into the sewing room.

Marta told Greg Maggie had appeared to be fine all day. She had told her that Mommy had gone to heaven, without her seeming terribly disturbed. Marta thought, too, that Maggie was unable to comprehend what was happening—for she loved her mommy so much, there was no way she could not be upset, if she understood.

After Marta left, Greg found Maggie in the

wooden rocker in the sewing room, reading and giggling as she rocked. This was puzzling to him. How could she be so happy?

The next day was the day of Lisa's visitation. Maggie was again with Marta. Greg had asked the funeral director if he could come to see Lisa late morning. He wanted time to be alone with her. He didn't want anyone there when he saw her the first time, as he knew he would break down. He dressed in his red lambskin shirt and black turtleneck that he knew Lisa loved so. Yes, it was a little out of season, as it was only late September. It was a cool day, and Greg had been unable to keep warm since Lisa died. He wondered how he could ever be prepared for seeing her. No man as young as he should have to see his wife like this—especially, when she was as precious to him as Lisa was to Greg.

The funeral director met him at the door, expressed his regards, and took him to Lisa. Greg was overwhelmed—more than overwhelmed! There she lay in the elegant ivory casket, looking so beautiful, as if she had drifted off to sleep—no pain, no worries. He reached over and took her hand. She felt so cold—so unreal—so dead! Tears were streaming down his face. He reached into his pocket, clutched his handkerchief, and wiped away the tears, repeatedly. He tried to hug Lisa. How do you hug your wife who is lying in a casket? He mimicked a hug, the best he could, as he kissed her lips. "My precious, precious Lisa. Don't leave me, Lisa. I need you!" He stood by her, trying to gain composure—wondering how he could get through this—how he could stand here greeting their friends and family. He finally managed to calm himself somewhat; made an attempt to squeeze her hand, and turned and left without looking back, knowing he would be back in a few hours. He had lost track of time and had no idea how long he had stayed. Time was irrelevant.

He hardly remembered driving home, where he sat in the parlor for quite some time—thinking, remembering. This room had been extra special to them. It was almost unbearable to think that he would never feel Lisa's closeness again, as he had experienced in front of this fireplace so many times before she became ill. This house was filled with memories. He could hear her talking and see her in every room.

Marta arrived with Maggie. She was dressed for the visitation, and as planned, stayed to help Maggie get dressed. Greg hadn't thought he could manage by himself—not yet. Lori had laid Maggie's clothes out earlier, a little pink knit suit Lisa had bought late summer. Lori wondered when she saw it, if Lisa bought it intentionally for her funeral.

Maggie seemed a bit quieter than normal. She ran into the sewing room when she first arrived, quietly looked around, then went back to be with Greg. She could see tears in his eyes and knew he was sad. Greg picked her up and hugged her. He was at a loss for words. His grasp on her, told her he was very upset. "Daddy, it's time for my bath. Marta will help me get dressed to go see Mommy." Greg put her down, and she ran toward Marta.

Marta rode to the funeral home with them. They were to have thirty minutes alone with Lisa before the visitation was to begin. Maggie took Greg's hand as they got out of the car. They slowly walked toward the door. Marta thought how proud Lisa would be of how handsome Greg looked in his dark gray suit. He had chosen a white dress shirt and the plum tie Lisa had bought for him, the same day she bought her plum suit. Greg was in no hurry to go in. He was afraid of his reaction and Maggie's, too. He knew this would also be terribly difficult for Marta, as she and Lisa had been close for so many years. As they were walking in, Lori and Steve drove up, and followed them in.

The room was dimly lit. The elegant ivory casket sat in the far corner of the large room. The room was scented with the fragrance of the many beautiful bouquets, plants, and baskets of flowers. The candelabras at each end of the casket gave off soft lighting, which accented Lisa's beauty. Greg, still holding Maggie's hand, led her to the casket.

Maggie stood quietly in front of the casket staring up at Lisa with her big blue eyes. She turned and looked at Greg, then Marta, then Lori and Steve. "Why is Mommy asleep in that pretty box?" she asked.

At that moment, no one was able to speak. The words seemed to stick in their throats. Marta was overcome by seeing Lisa; the embroidered "Our precious love", took her by surprise. She had never seen a casket so special and so appropriate for Lisa.

Greg remembered Lisa's words, "Be strong for Maggie."

He then answered Maggie's question, "Mommy isn't asleep, honey. Remember, we told you she died and has gone to heaven to live with Jesus?"

Maggie was puzzled, so puzzled she said no more. She was back and forth between the four of them, not knowing quite what to think. "Mommy's asleep, I know she is," she told Lori.

Greg had been undecided whether Maggie should even attend the visitation. It was difficult for him to make any decisions. He knew only one thing for sure. Lisa was no longer alive. He had lost his precious Lisa. Marta and Lori had talked and decided Maggie should go to the visitation with them.

Many people filed past Lisa's casket—so many tears and expressions of sympathy. Somehow, Greg got through it.

Maggie was quiet as they drove back to the house. She was the first one out of the car. As soon as Greg unlocked the door, she ran into the sewing room and hopped into the wooden rocker with a book. She was soon giggling as if nothing had happened. Greg could hear her from the other rooms, giggling as she read to her babies.

*

Greg awoke early the next morning, the day of the funeral—if he slept at all. He felt he hadn't. How could he sleep knowing he was to say his final good-byes to his one and only love—his precious love? He and Lisa had agreed what they had found with each other was something most couples never find in a lifetime. Their love for one another was obvious to all. They had maintained that special glow throughout their marriage. Many couples lose this early in their marriage, if they have had it at all. Maggie's birth had enhanced their love. She was such a beautiful child, always well behaved and loving. They had spoken of this many times, how she seemed to radiate from the love the two of them shared. She lived in a home with more love than most little children. How could it be any different, with the love Greg and Lisa felt for each other? This had always made life so enjoyable. They knew only love—never arguing, never even a cross word. With a home like this, Maggie couldn't be anything other than loveable.

Greg thought of how much they had wanted a brother or sister for Maggie; how Lisa had thought she was pregnant when she first became ill with the cancer. Oh, how wrong she was—the disappointment she must have felt. Throughout her illness she remained strong, never seeming to feel sorry for herself. She was the strongest and most wonderful person Greg had ever known. To say good-bye to her was unthinkable. How could he do this? How would he get through it? Maggie's reaction was nagging at him. How could she remain happy and giggly throughout all of this?

Marta arrived early to help Greg get Maggie ready for the funeral. Few words were spoken. Neither was up to talking, each was deep in thought, when Maggie surprised them both.

"Is Mommy coming with us today?"

Somewhat shocked, after a hesitation, Marta answered, "Yes, Mommy will be there."

They arrived at the funeral home forty-five minutes before the funeral. Only family was to be there at this time. Greg, Marta, and Lori all had a difficult time.

Maggie appeared more puzzled than before. "Why is Mommy still asleep?" she asked Greg. She asked that he lift her up so she could see her mommy. Maggie didn't take her eyes off Lisa for quite some time. Eventually, she told Greg he could put her down, and added, "Mommy must be very sleepy."

When it came time to say the final good-bye before going to the church, Steve took Maggie on ahead of the rest. She didn't need to see how badly Greg and the ladies were going to react.

Greg found it unbearable to say good-bye. He leaned down and kissed Lisa, giving her a mock hug, as he said, "Bye doll," tears streaming down his face.

Marta and Lori each walked beside him, practically holding him up.

They got into the limo with Steve and Maggie. It was a short ride to St. Mary's church.

Maggie wondered why they were stopping at the church. After all, it wasn't Sunday. As they got out of the car, Maggie saw the pallbearers carrying the casket into the church. "Is that Mommy's pretty bed? It looks different. It looks like a pretty toy box with the lid closed. Where's Mommy? Why are we sitting in the front? We usually sit in the middle of the church. Why is Mommy's bed in the aisle beside us? Why is Daddy crying?" Maggie was glad when the service was over. She heard many muffled cries. Nothing made any sense to her.

As they drove into the cemetery, Maggie was even more puzzled. "Why is the man bringing us to the place with all the big rocks with names on them? I have been here before with mommy. We put flowers by the rock with Grandma Nicholson's name on it. Why is Mommy's pretty bed here?"

Maggie was even more confused when they got back into the car and went to the church for lunch. "Where is Mommy's bed now? Daddy, I want to go home and see Mommy!" she cried. "Daddy, Daddy, where is Mommy? I want to go see Mommy!"

Greg took Maggie home and tried to explain to her how Mommy was with Jesus, as they had discussed earlier. Maggie cried and cried. She ran from Greg's arms into the sewing room, where she and Lisa had spent so many hours. She climbed into the rocking chair and began to rock rhythmically. She soon stopped crying and fell fast asleep.

With Maggie quiet, Greg slipped away from the crowded house full of well-meaning friends and family. The horrible emptiness in his heart seemed to multiply by each second, with no place to be alone. Relatives were looking at a picture album, laughing, and remembering the good times. This seemed so heartless to Greg. Lisa was gone. They were laughing. How could they?

He drove into the cemetery and stopped a few feet from Lisa's grave. The grave had been closed; the sod was carefully put back in place, and the flowers were on the grave, some already beginning to wilt. Greg knelt in front of the small pewter marker that read Lisa Margaret Carrington   Wrights Funeral Home. Here he was, finally alone with Lisa, away from the many relatives back at the house. He lay on the grave beside the flowers, stretching his arms out over the grave as he sobbed, "Lisa, Lisa, Lisa...how did this happen? My precious baby." He wanted to hold her and kiss away the pain. Even though he knew she was no longer in pain, it was extremely difficult to believe she could no longer feel. He and Lisa were quite religious, each believing in eternal life. He knew in his heart that she was now in a better place. He wanted to be selfish. He wanted her back. After a while, the tears subsided. He got up on his knees and took two pink rose buds from the casket spray for him and Maggie. He slowly stood up and walked away, passing the graves next to Lisa's, with the headstone marked Nicholson—Doris Margaret and Claude Henry, his heart heavier with each step. One thing he knew was that Lisa was now with her mom and dad. She had hardly known her dad, as he had passed away when she was only three.

Greg must have driven around for hours. When he returned home, only Marta was there with Maggie. The house felt cold and empty. Maggie was helping Marta clean up the kitchen. There was an abundance of food left—food that had been brought in by so many wonderful friends and neighbors. Marta had decided to freeze some of it for Greg to use later.

Marta sensed Greg wanted to be alone with Maggie, so she left as soon as she had the food taken care of. Greg sat remembering—so many thoughts of Lisa. The emptiness was setting in. Maggie was quite calm now. She sat quietly thinking over the day's events. She knew everyone was telling her Mommy was with Jesus now. What did that mean? Why was she always asleep in that pretty bed at the church and the place with the big rocks? There was much confusion in her little head. Greg tucked her into bed and sat by her side until she fell asleep, which took much longer than usual. He walked down the spiral staircase and sat in front of the fireplace in the parlor for what must have been hours.

What now?

He kept hearing the paramedic's words, "Mr. Carrington… I'm sorry… she's gone… she's gone… she's gone…" The words kept ringing in his ears. He felt he would go crazy if they didn't stop.

He knelt down to light the fireplace. The house seemed chilly and empty. He couldn't get warm. After the fireplace was aglow, he noticed the sofa pillows were on the floor, exactly where he and Lisa used to place them when they lay in front of the fireplace. He lay down and put his head on one of the pillows. He began to feel warmth surrounding him. Suddenly, his lips felt as if he was being kissed. Oh, such soft, wonderful lips—Lisa's lips. His belt was being unbuckled and his pants were sliding down his legs. He could almost feel Lisa's fingers inside the elastic of his briefs, removing them. He became aroused at the thought of it.

I must be asleep and dreaming.

He lay there stripped naked from the waist down, feeling aroused and somewhat confused at the same time. Then, one by one the buttons popped off of his shirt. The shirt slipped off first one shoulder, then the other. *This has to be a dream. There is no way clothes take themselves off.* Soon, he had a sensation of weight on his thighs and his erection felt as if it was being guided, until it felt warmth and enclosure. *What the heck?* He was now feeling wonderfully aroused. *No, it can't be!* He reached out, wrapped his arms around Lisa and began to move in rhythm with her. Oh, how he had missed her! How he had missed moments like this. He wanted to make this moment last forever. She was now riding him faster. Each stroke became more intense. He imagined he could hear her moaning. She climaxed, falling limp on his chest, her sensuous breasts upon his bare chest. She was there embracing his body.

He carried her upstairs to his bed, their bed, where he lay there holding her, never wanting to let go. He knew if this was for real, she could not stay. He wanted to make love to her one last time. He rolled her onto her back and rose above her, settling between her thighs and again made love to her. He wondered how this was possible, making love to a spirit, his beautiful Lisa, now a spirit. This was difficult to grasp. He would enjoy her warmth and love while he could. He thought he could hear her pleasure, her climax, just moments before he deposited his love inside her. At least he thought he had. He lay down beside her. As he lay there, he could feel her wonderful breasts against his bare skin. He laid his head upon them, thinking, *If only this was for real.*

For a moment he saw an outline of a glowing figure. Yes, it was Lisa in a beautiful spirit form. She was radiant. Sometime in the middle of the night, he fell asleep embracing Lisa's spirit form.

He awoke the next morning remembering what he had felt the night before, the most beautiful dream one could ever have, or was it? He longed so for Lisa. The dream had made him miss her more.

Five

The house was far too quiet these days. Losing Lisa was the most difficult thing Greg had ever experienced in his life. The days were long and painful. At times, it seemed as if it was all a bad dream, with the reality of it hitting him in the next moment. The house now seemed huge.

Maggie was spending most of her time in the sewing room. Greg was unable to interest her in anything else for more than a few minutes at a time. She would sit for hours reading to her babies, talking, and giggling. Greg had moved an easy chair from the parlor into this room to be closer to Maggie. He had to admit, there was a certain warmth about this room. He would attempt to read, his thoughts always going back to Lisa. He had rethought their life together starting from the first day he met her in geometry class, to their first prom, to the day they married, to the day she became pregnant with Maggie, to the day they bought the house, to the day she got sick, to that horrible day when she died.

The dream he had after Lisa's funeral was always there, flashing through his mind, along with all the memories. He went to bed each night hoping this night would be the night he would again dream of her. The phrase, it is better to have loved and lost, than never to have loved at all, rang through his mind. He now was beginning to doubt that phrase, because if he had never known such a love, he wouldn't miss Lisa so much. He knew there would never be another Lisa, never be another love like he had with her. The days were difficult. There seemed to be little to live for. Marta and Lori had tried to help him. They had brought in food, and Marta had come to the house and prepared some meals. Neither knew how to draw him out of his depression. His work was suffering. He knew he had to pull himself together—but how?

The phone rang. It was Marta. "Greg, have you looked outside?"

"No, I can't say as I have, not in the past couple of hours. I've been sitting here trying to catch up on some reading. I'm not getting too far though, my concentration isn't there."

"It's snowing. It's coming down in big, beautiful flakes. You know…Chestnut opened recently. This snow makes me want to get my skis out and brush up. It has been a long time; I didn't get out last year. My business was requiring too much of my time. I haven't been since…" Her words trailed off as she almost slipped and said she hadn't been since she and Lisa went the winter before last. "I'm afraid I'm really rusty. I could use your support. Do you suppose you could go with me Saturday?"

Greg, reluctantly, agreed to help her. He still wasn't into much of anything—it had only been two months since Lisa's death. Skiing was something he and Lisa did together. Actually, he and Lisa had done almost everything together. Everything he did, reminded him of her because of this.

What Greg didn't know, was that Marta and Lori had devised this plan. Lori had already asked Greg if they could have Maggie for the weekend. They wanted Maggie to come see their new puppy and help with choosing a name for her. Marta had always had a bit of a crush on Greg and she knew Lisa had known this. It had never bothered Lisa, as Marta was her best friend and she would never betray her. Greg never knew about this crush. The three of them were friends, nothing more. After Lisa's death, Lori decided to tell Marta of Lisa's wish. Marta had no idea of this, although it didn't actually surprise her. When Lori suggested the skiing outing, Marta wasn't so sure it was a good idea, as Lisa hadn't been gone that long. It didn't seem right. Lori had convinced her that Greg was not doing well, and he needed help to bring him out of this. He needed a friend, and for now that was all it need be, a companion to help him through this difficult time. Lori had finally convinced her to ask Greg to go skiing with her.

After talking to Marta, Greg decided to go out to the carriage house to check on the condition of his skis. He remembered having stored them in the loft of the stable. He felt a bit unsettled about returning to the stable and even more so about going into the loft. He didn't like leaving Maggie alone in the house. Therefore, he placed her old baby monitor by her bed. He grabbed the receiver from the parlor on his way out to the carriage house. He knew if she needed him, he would hear her. The night was dark and cold. Winter was definitely setting in. A chill went through his body at the thought of returning to the stable. He hadn't been in this area of the carriage house in some time. He had tried to block the mysterious, red substance from his mind. He had enough to think about with Lisa's passing.

As he entered the carriage house and walked toward the stable, an eerie feeling came over him. Perhaps he should have waited until daylight to venture into this part of the carriage house. He was relieved to find the stable free from any crimson fluid. As he climbed the ladder to the loft, the eeriness intensified—the cold chill turned frigid. He slowly raised the trap door. A stench, the smell of rotting flesh, hit him immediately. He climbed into the loft, making sure the trap door was secured open, in case he had to make a quick escape. He grabbed the flashlight, which he kept by the trap door, and shined it into the loft. Sure enough, the sticky substance was back. It covered a large part of the loft floor; the smell was extremely offensive. Greg grabbed his skis and fled through the trap door and down the ladder.

As he ran to the house, he remembered he left the monitor receiver in the stable. There was no way he would go back there tonight. He left the skis in the servants' entrance and ran up the steps to Maggie's room. She was fast asleep. He turned the monitor off, so nothing could be heard in the stable. There was no other word for his feelings except spooked—and no explanation to be found for this. What the hell was happening? He thought of Lisa and was so glad she never knew of any of this—so glad she didn't have to feel what he was feeling tonight. He knew that he must return to the stable soon to rid it of the substance and the stench, before it consumed the entire carriage house. He had left in such a hurry that the trap door was left open. This made him feel even more uncomfortable.

The next morning, after he saw Maggie off to school, he again went back to the carriage house stable and climbed the ladder into the loft. Much to his disbelief, there was no red, sticky substance—no stench. This was even more puzzling to him than the appearance of the substance. He grabbed the receiver and walked back to the house rather stunned.

Needless to say, he didn't accomplish much at work that day. He was glad Maggie was going to Lori's for the night, as he was uneasy with her being at the house, at this time. Lori picked Maggie up from school and dropped by the house long enough to help her pack a suitcase. Before leaving the house, Maggie ran into the sewing room. Her attachment to the sewing room was a mystery to all. She was in and right out, almost as if she had to tell it good-bye.

Steve greeted them at the farm with an adorable little, white bichon frise puppy. It was love at first sight. She was wearing a tiny pink collar with a tiny silver bell that jingled as she ran about. Maggie giggled as she played with her.

Lori wished Lisa could see her so happy with the little pup. Then she thought, *Well, maybe she can.*

"I will call her Tinker Bell," giggled Maggie, "for the way her little bell jingles like Tinker Bell in Peter Pan."

"Oh, how cute! Why didn't we think of that, Steve?" They had known Maggie would come up with a cute name.

Maggie soon wore Tinker Bell out. She fell asleep on Maggie's lap.

Greg spent the evening alone. He was consumed with the red substance issue. Never had anything mystified him so. How could the substance have disappeared? The stench had been grossly overwhelming, yet it was gone a short time later. He had thought it would take an extremely strong air freshener to rid the stable of such a stench. It made no sense, but he was grateful he didn't have to battle the odor or clean up the mess.

He cleaned his skis and prepared them for the next day, never going near the stable. He was determined he wouldn't go near the stable for some time now, if he could avoid it. The night was long. He needed to confide in someone about this, soon. So far he had kept it to himself. He had hesitated to tell anyone, thinking it was too unbelievable. He wouldn't believe it himself, if he hadn't seen it with his own eyes.

*

Greg was up early the next morning. He hadn't slept well. How could he, with the reoccurrence of the red fluid? It weighed heavily on his mind. Skiing, now, was a welcome idea. Maybe this would keep his mind off of this nightmare for a while, but would skiing make him think about Lisa more? Life certainly was not easy these days.

The Tahoe was parked in the carriage house. Greg didn't relish the idea of entering the building to retrieve his vehicle. He tried to convince himself it wouldn't be a problem, as the stable was at the other end of the carriage house. He went out early and cleared the drive of the four inches of new snow and proceeded to go into the carriage house. It showed no signs of any problem. He quickly backed the Tahoe out, closed, and locked the doors. Maybe he would start leaving the

Tahoe out. Why should he put himself through this every time he needed the vehicle? He returned to the house and drank another cup of coffee, while he waited for time to pass. It was too early to pick Marta up.

He drove into Marta's drive a few minutes before eight. She flew out the door, wearing a sky blue ski jacket and pants, with a blue snowflake design ski cap. Grabbing her skis off the porch, like a small child, she shuffled her feet through the snow, as she walked toward Greg. Oh, how she loved new fallen snow. Greg took her skis from her, raised the back hatch on the Tahoe, and laid them inside.

"How about if I clean that sidewalk off for you?"

"And take the neighbor kid's profit from him? We have an understanding that whenever it snows, he is to come over and shovel my walks. It's early yet. You know how young kids are. They like to sleep in on Saturdays. He will be here soon, I'm sure."

Marta couldn't help but think how handsome Greg looked in his navy and white ski suit. He definitely was a dreamy looking guy. Everything about him was dreamy, in her eyes. He locked the hatch and opened the passenger door for Marta. As they drove off, he was thinking how strange it was to have Marta in the seat beside him, instead of Lisa. Would he ever get used to Lisa being gone?

It was a short drive to the ski resort. The parking lot was already filling. Greg was glad they had their own skis and boots, so they wouldn't have to go through that line. They checked in and got lockers, put their boots on, bought ski lift tickets, and were on the ski lift in just a few short minutes, while others were still waiting to rent skis.

The view from the ski lift was breathtaking, as

always, as Chestnut is perched high on a bluff overlooking the expansive Mississippi river. It looks as if you could ski right to the edge of the river. Of the seventeen trails, Marta had chosen Old Main, as she needed to brush up on her skiing a bit before she tackled one of the more advanced trails.

As Marta went down slightly ahead of Greg, he was thinking, "That's rusty?" She even skied like Lisa. They had skied together so much they had begun to ski alike. They had always loved the jumps—one trying to outdo the other—although not really. They were always the best of friends. They had always had so much fun together, regardless of what they were doing. Watching Marta's beautiful style, as she glided down the mountain, made him realize how much she even looked like Lisa. She had the same trim build and the same color hair, although Marta's was a little longer than Lisa had kept hers.

Marta rapidly went through all the intermediate trails, until she felt she was now ready for the Eagle, which was one of the most difficult and advanced slopes.

"Are you sure you are up for the Eagle?" Greg asked. "Remember, you're rusty!" He laughed, as he spoke. She definitely was not rusty!

Would you look at that! Marta thought to herself, as she heard Greg laughing. It was the first real laugh she had heard since Lisa died. Yes, skiing was a wonderful idea.

They both were having a marvelous time. The day passed quickly, until they were soon in the Tahoe headed back home.

"Greg, I have been thinking about your third floor. You know, I have never seen it. Lisa was always going to take me up there. We never seemed to get around to it. Do you suppose you could give me the tour today?"

"I don't see why not. Actually, I have never been up there. The realtor said it wasn't livable in its present state, and we didn't need the room. I started to check it out several times. There was so much going on that I never got up there. I had enough on my mind with the renovations for the downstairs, then the move, and then…" he hesitated a minute, "then with Lisa so sick my attention was on her. One day she wanted us to go up there, but she decided she was too weak to take those steep narrow steps." They pulled into the drive just as the sun was setting.

Greg lit the logs in the parlor fireplace, so they could warm up and dry off before going up to the mansard. He then poured some wine for the two of them, a mild chardonnay, to relax by.

Marta had never been up the back stairs, which led to a small sitting room. From there they opened the door to the enclosed third floor stairs. As Greg opened the door, they both detected a stench, which was all too familiar to Greg. He switched on the rather primitive light to see the familiar red stuff.

"What the heck is that?" screamed Marta.

Greg explained to her it had appeared twice before. He was glad to be able to share this secret, which he had kept to himself long enough. He hurried down the steep back stairs to get some rags from the basement, with Marta close at his heels. There was no way he was leaving her upstairs by herself!

Once the substance was cleaned up, they climbed the steep stairs to the third floor. As they approached the large main room, they could see the disarray of many stored items. Marta was anxious to rummage through these items. They were old, and more than likely there were some valuables in some of the boxes. Regardless, there was sure to be some interesting items. Marta was surprised at the ten foot high ceilings. From the outside, one would have never known the ceilings were so high. There was substantial space here, with four bedrooms plus this large room that more than likely had been a sitting room for the servants.

Marta opened a large closet to find many old framed portraits. She studied each and every one, becoming very interested in one—a young girl not much older than her teens, possibly early twenties. She was lovely and very elegantly dressed in a rose-colored gown. Carefully, Marta removed it from the frame and turned it over to find something scribbled on the back. It was smudged and illegible. This wasn't surprising, as the old quill ink pens used ink that wasn't permanent. Marta became more and more interested in this portrait, wanting to learn the facts about this young girl who was so beautiful. Who she was and what became of her were of utmost interest to Marta.

After several hours, she and Greg returned to the second floor sitting room. Greg agreed to allow her to search later for any details of this girl. For now, Marta wanted to hang this portrait in the spare bedroom. Greg found a nail and hanger in his office, and they chose a spot on the wall. It complemented the already enchanting room.

They returned to the parlor to talk. Marta offered to prepare dinner for the two of them. She found a couple of small steaks in the freezer, which she placed under the broiler. While the steak was cooking, she made a lettuce salad. Greg put two potatoes in the microwave. They talked about the events of the evening, mainly the fowl smelling substance, the condition of the third floor, and the portrait. As an interior decorator, Marta had many ideas how they could clean the rooms up and decorate that floor.

"What do I need more room for, Marta? This house is huge as it is. Lisa and I talked of opening that floor up someday as guest quarters, after we had more children." For a second, he looked as if he would cry. The memories of the plans he and Lisa had, were too painful to think about yet. His mind wandered to how happy she had been, thinking she was pregnant, when in reality she was in the early stages of cancer.

"It would be fun and something to do," Marta answered. "You know me, how I love to decorate. You could rent it out."

"I don't know about that. One must enter our private living quarters to gain access to the stairs. Sure, back in the time the house was built the servants lived up there. They were in and out of the house anyway. I don't know how I would feel about strangers entering the floor housing our bedrooms. I suppose if we installed a door at the end of the hall and kept it locked it might work. Except, then we wouldn't be able to use the back stairs. As it is now, I can come and go easily to the carriage house and my workshop. That is, if I ever open my workshop. I'm just not sure now that I want to. First, I must find out what is causing the red crap to appear."

Marta felt a chill go through her body at the thought of the mysterious substance.

They dismissed the subject and began discussing the portrait. "Would you mind if I come back tomorrow and look for any information that might be there as to whom this young girl is, or was, as the case must be?" Marta asked.

"If you like, I have nothing planned for tomorrow. Maggie will still be at the farm."

It was approaching 11:00 PM, so Greg took Marta home. He hated coming home to the big empty house. It had been pleasant having Marta there with him. She was such a fun gal and so much like Lisa, in so many ways.

As Greg was getting into bed, he thought he heard the cries of a baby. *Not again,* he thought. *Please, not this on top of everything else.* He listened carefully and decided it was his imagination. As he was drifting off to sleep, he heard muffled cries. This time he was sure—it was the same baby's cry that he had heard so many months previously.

*

The next morning, Greg was sitting in the parlor reading the paper, or rather staring at it, when Marta arrived. He hadn't expected her quite so early. It was obvious she was anxious to begin her search for the identity of the beautiful young girl. Or was it that she wanted another peek at the third floor mansard? How she loved redecorating. It was nice for Greg to see such a warm smile so early in the morning.

"Hi, I'm not too early, I hope."

"No, I've been up for hours. Come on in. Would you like some coffee? Or some breakfast?"

"No, thanks, I ate earlier. I hope you don't mind I'm so early. I'm anxious to rummage through the mansard, to see if we can find anything about the girl in the picture." Marta was her usual bubbly self.

"Sure, hon, no problem. It's nice to have such

lovely company so early in the morning…or anytime really. It keeps me from feeling sorry for myself. Maggie is company, just not the kind I need. She spends so much of her time in the sewing room reading, rocking, and talking to herself that I see less and less of her. I don't understand why she enjoys reading so much anymore. Maybe it's her way of coping with Lisa's death. I guess I should just be glad she is happy and healthy. In time, maybe she will wean herself from this phase."

As Greg opened the door to the third floor, the stench hit them both. Sure enough, the red, sticky substance was back again! "Oh my God no! Why does this keep happening to me? I wish we could find some answers to this in that rummage up there. There must be a reason. Something tells me I will never know the answer. The question is, how do I get it to stop? And…what the hell is it? The entire thing is so insane…" His words faded off as he hurried down the stairs to get some rags.

Marta backed away from the stairs and stepped into the guest room to look at the portrait again. She was so startled with what she saw that she knocked over a vase on the table in front of the portrait. It came crashing to the floor. Greg came rushing in. He had heard the crash, when he was coming up the stairs.

"What was that?" he yelled. When he reached Marta, he instantly knew, as pieces of the broken vase were scattered about the floor. As his eyes followed the wall, he noticed the girl in the portrait had tears in her eyes, and the paint below her eyes appeared wet and shiny.

"What the hell?" Greg was totally bewildered. "What next? Is this house haunted or what?" He put his arms around Marta and drew her close. He could feel her trembling.

"I'm okay, really," Marta finally was able to speak. She had been enjoying the warmth of his arms around her. She almost hated to speak up, not wanting it to end. She had been attracted to him for so long, thinking for years he was off limits, because he was married to Lisa. Could things possibly be opening up for her now? *No*, she thought, *It's only the circumstances of today.*

"Let me clean this mess up and the one on the stairs; then let's go downstairs for a while." He felt she needed to relax and try to forget what she saw. He knew it would be impossible for either of them to forget, but relaxing with Marta suddenly sounded wonderful to him. He hadn't wanted to let go of her.

"I'd rather not, I've been too anxious to get up to the mansard again. I'm fine. Let's not let this stop us."

Greg hurriedly cleaned up the red substance and carried the dirty rags out to the barrel. He grabbed a broom from the cellar way on his way back through the hallway and returned to Marta to find her staring at the picture again. The picture was now totally dry.

Greg was puzzled, "What did you use to dry it off?"

"Nothing, I haven't touched the picture!"

"It's a good thing we were here together, for both of us to see this. One of us alone wouldn't have believed our eyes. We may have dismissed it as our imagination. Things get crazier and crazier around here. I'm glad you're in this with me—well, not for your sake. I really hate it that you're involved, but I was going nuts keeping all this to myself."

"Maybe we can go to the library and find some books on hauntings. Possibly, we could find something on the computer. If we Google *hauntings* maybe we can turn up something," Marta suggested.

Greg swept up the pieces of the broken vase and dumped it in a wastebasket in his office.

"Are you sure you are up to this?" he asked Marta, as he propped the broom up beside the mansard stairway.

"I'm beginning to wonder, but yes, let's do this before I change my mind."

Marta quickly became involved in going through all the treasures of the mansard. She seemed to forget about the earlier occurrences. She was in her glory rummaging through box after box that had been left by earlier tenants. Greg also was seriously searching through items, mostly books, hoping to find answers. He was concentrating mainly on information that could lead him to answers about the red, sticky substance. They searched for hours. As they were ready to break for lunch, Marta let out a yell. "Greg! Look at this!"

Greg rushed to her side, "What is it, Mart?"

"Look! It's an old family bible. In the back it lists names of a family. Do you suppose it's the family that lived here years ago?"

"Quite possibly, as it's here in this house. Who else would it be?"

"I need to study this. Did you say something about lunch?" Marta asked.

"I sure did, I'm absolutely starved."

They went down the stairs to the sitting room. Marta noticed Greg looking a little puzzled, "Something wrong, Greg?"

"I could have sworn I propped the broom up here."

"Yes, you did, I saw you. It didn't fall down the

stairs did it?"

Greg rushed down the stairs with Marta close behind. They searched the servants' hallway. There was no broom in sight. Greg was determined to find it. He ran back up the stairs and looked again—nothing. He returned looking a bit spooked, "I'm going to put a lock on that stairway door. It makes me uncomfortable."

Marta was studying the bible when Greg asked, "How hungry are you? Do you think you could eat some lasagna? There is a place close by that delivers."

"Sounds wonderful to me! Actually, I'm famished!"

"I would suggest we go out, except I'm afraid we are both a little dusty dirty from all the dust flying around up there." He dialed the phone, placed the order, and returned to Marta at the kitchen table. He placed his hands on her shoulders and began gently massaging them. "How about moving to the parlor until the delivery arrives?"

"Sure, sounds like a good idea. Kitchen chairs aren't the most relaxing."

The fireplace was warm and glowing. Greg sat on the sofa and motioned for her to sit beside him, which she happily did. He put his arm around her and drew her close. She laid her head on his shoulder while they sat quietly watching the glowing fire. Greg was wishing he had brought some wine in. The moment seemed to call for it.

"Mart, do you think Lisa would mind us here like this?"

"I know she wouldn't, Greg."

"How is that?"

"Greg, she had a talk with Lori before she died."

"What do you mean...a talk?" Greg was quite curious.

"She told Lori she didn't want you grieving your life away. She wanted Lori to encourage you and I to become friends."

"You serious?" he was quite surprised.

"I certainly wouldn't joke about something like this. Actually, she wanted us to become more than friends."

"So, what were her wishes?" Greg coaxed.

"She wanted us to become interested in one another. She... she..."

"She what? Please tell me, Mart."

"She wanted us to fall in love. She wanted us to be together."

"Are you saying what I think you are? She wanted us to marry?" Greg couldn't believe what he was hearing.

"Yes, that's what she told Lori."

"What would have given her such an idea?"

"Greg, she didn't want you to be lonely...and..."

"And..."

"This is difficult for me, Greg. Lisa was my best friend. But, she did have certain reasons for wanting us to be together, one that you don't know."

"What do you mean?" Greg was even more curious now.

"Greg, you know Lisa and I were friends dating back to high school."

"Of course, and we used to double date with what's his name, Dwight was it? What ever became of him?"

"I'm not really sure. I think he moved away. I was never really interested in him. He knew that, and Lisa did, too."

"And why not? He seemed like a very nice guy, and

a fun guy to be around," Greg continued.

"I had other interests," Marta replied.

"And what might they have been?"

"Please, Greg…"

"Please, what Mart?"

"Please, don't put me on the spot. Talk to Lori, she knows," Marta suggested.

"Why should I ask Lori, when you have the answer?"

"Greg, it's just hard for me to talk to you about it."

"Now you really have me curious. Out with it Mart." He began stroking her hair, convincing her to explain.

"Greg, honey, I have had feelings for you since way back then…and Lisa knew it."

"And no one ever told me? Why didn't I know?"

"Because…you and Lisa were an item from the beginning. There was no way I was going to butt in."

"I should have known." He drew Marta closer and kissed her gently on the lips, then sat with her in his embrace until the doorbell rang. The delivery had arrived. Greg took her hand and led her, glowing, to the kitchen.

They both agreed the lasagna had been a good idea. It was delicious. Marta cleared the table off and washed the few dishes.

"Now what?" Greg inquired of Marta.

Marta really wanted to return to where they left off, but she didn't want to rush Greg. "Let's go back to the mansard and see what more we can find. The bible lists names, but really doesn't give us the name of the girl in the picture."

Greg agreed. He still hadn't found any answer to why the mysterious, red substance kept appearing. He had his doubts they would ever find any information as to why this was happening or what it was. They slowly climbed the back stairs, as neither was in a hurry for any more surprises. Greg hesitated before opening the stair door. "Whew," he sighed. There was no more red stuff or anything mysterious.

They decided to begin looking in one of the bedrooms. Much to their surprise, in the first one they entered, there they found the broom propped up against the wall.

"Is that the broom, Greg?"

He bent down to examine it. "Sure looks like it to me. It has the same scuffmark on the handle, same brand, and everything. How the hell did it get up here? We haven't even been in this room yet. This is a little unsettling to me. Maybe we should go back downstairs." Greg grabbed a large box, "I'll take this and we can sort through it downstairs."

Marta picked up a smaller box and followed Greg down the stairs. They sat at the kitchen table examining the contents of both. There were many pictures in the boxes; many were dated and labeled with names. Some of the ink had been smeared. Greg came across a picture he felt resembled the beautiful girl. He held it up for Marta to see.

"I think it's her," she said. "I definitely wouldn't forget those eyes. I can't read the name, can you?"

"No, it's smudged. Keep looking, maybe there is another one here," Greg said.

After a couple of hours, they finished going through the boxes. Their eyes were feeling strained. It would be dark soon. They didn't care to return to the mansard after dark.

"I'd like to run to the hardware store and get a lock

for that door. Care to come along, Mart?"

"Sure, we need to brush some of this dust off ourselves first."

After they stepped into the back hall and did just that, Greg gently brushed the dust off Marta's hair, drew her close to him, and kissed her—a long, gentle kiss that could have easily turned into a long, passionate kiss. Marta put her arms around him and held him tightly. She had longed to do this for so long.

"Time to get our coats on and get to the hardware store before they close." Greg helped her with her coat and opened the jeep door for her. They would take her vehicle since it was blocking his Tahoe. "I'll drive." He went around and got behind the wheel. Marta handed him the keys. The hardware store was only a few blocks away. Greg found the lock he wanted, and they were back home in a few short minutes.

He installed the lock while Marta sat in the upstairs sitting room—watching, thinking of all the years she had admired and loved him. She so hoped Lisa's wish would eventually come true. She and Greg enjoyed skiing, but skiing was a long way from the relationship that she dreamed of. Greg was tired, as he hadn't slept well lately.

When they went down to the parlor, he lay back on the pillow at the end of the sofa and looked over at Marta sitting at the other end. She was certainly a lovely gal. He began to mentally undress her. He felt this was wrong, especially so soon after Lisa's death— nonetheless, the thoughts were there. He missed Lisa's warmth—her love. Desires began to swell within him. He reached for Marta's hand and pulled her close. Their lips met in that passionate kiss. She started to pull away, thinking it was too soon. He pulled her closer, and began rubbing her back through her shirt. He wanted so much to be under her shirt. Their tongues danced. Desires increased. He wanted to feel her breasts...to see them. When he could no longer resist, his hands found their way under her shirt. Marta was breathing heavily. He could no longer fight his own desires. With fingers fumbling, he unfastened her bra and reached around to feel her breasts. She was quickly succumbing to him. His heart pumping rapidly, he raised her shirt to see the most beautiful D breasts, so firm, so perfect, and so inviting. He looked up at Marta for approval. Her eyes seemed to say yes. He began to fondle and enjoy her breasts. Her mind was beginning to cloud over. Greg could tell he had her. He picked up the phone and dialed. Marta wondered why. She soon knew when she heard him asking what time they would be bringing Maggie home. "Okay, eight is quite alright. I'll see you then." He turned to Marta, "They aren't bringing Maggie home for a couple of hours yet." He took his shirt off and pulled her close. Her shirt lay rippled above her breasts. "May I?" he whispered, as he began to pull her shirt over her head.

She nodded in approval. Oh, how wonderful her awesome breasts felt against his bare chest. As they lay there, skin-to-skin, desires arose rapidly—each wanting—fighting their desires. Eventually, Greg could resist no longer. He slipped his hand inside her jeans and reached under her panties. With the first touch, he knew she wanted him every bit as much as he wanted her. He slowly removed her jeans, and began kissing his way down. Her breathing quickened. It was then that he unzipped his pants and showed her just how much he desired her.

Sweet, merciful heaven, Marta thought to herself, *Is it*

possible to have too much of a good thing?

There she lay with her midnight blue, bikini panties begging to be removed. Greg obliged, and laid his hand against her inner thigh, as a motion for her to spread her thighs to let him in. He ran his fingers slowly through her silky, brown, pubic hair, her love nest.

Her heart was racing with anticipation. The moment she had been dreaming of all these years was about to happen. Her heart raced faster. Greg's thoughts were on Marta only. Lisa was set aside for now, as he laid Marta back and slowly but eagerly guided his arousal into her readiness. He was gentle, telling himself he didn't want to hurt her, knowing nothing of her past experience. As she took him totally, he began to move gently at first, then faster, as she began making wonderful sounds of pleasure. One last thrust and it was over.

They lay in disbelief of what had just happened. Only yesterday they had gone skiing, being just friends.

"Could some good have come from the mysteries of this house?" Greg asked himself. Was this that just happened all out of need? He had so missed what he and Lisa had. He loved Lisa. How could he betray her and have sex with her best friend such a short time after her death? Two months was not nearly long enough. Why had he let this happen? Then he thought of Lisa's dying wish that Marta had told him about. Would Lisa understand if she had been looking down from above? Sure, she wanted them to be together. Would she have wanted this to happen so soon? Would she doubt his love for her, if he could betray her so now?

"Marta, we had better get our clothes on. Steve and Lori will be bringing Maggie soon. We really should be doing something about some supper. You hungry?"

"Now that you mention it, yes, I am."

"How does pizza sound to you? There really isn't much here in the house."

"Pizza is fine, Greg."

Marta could sense a change—some regret—some reluctance. "Greg, it's okay what just happened. Lisa would be happy for us. She understands. I know she does. After all, it was her wish." Marta seemed to be trying to convince herself of this, as much as she was trying to comfort Greg.

"I know Mart. I just can't help feeling a little disturbed about it happening this soon—as if I didn't really love Lisa."

"Greg, hon, I know you loved Lisa with all your heart. You loved her immensely, and you still do. Sometimes it's difficult to understand how things happen. Just know that I understand. And…Greg, what just happened was wonderful." She leaned over and kissed him—a gentle loving kiss. "Please, don't over think this. Be happy we were able to enjoy each other. So, what kind of pizza are we ordering?"

Marta was cleaning up the few dishes when Maggie came bouncing in. "Hi, Marta, you should see the new puppy. Her name is Tinker Bell. She is so much fun! I wish I had a puppy like her. Did you save any pizza for me?" Then she ran into the sewing room, flipped on the light, said something, and ran back into the kitchen.

Marta wondered what that was all about. She was reluctant to question her. Maggie eyed the piece of pizza and glass of milk Marta had set out for her. Luckily, Greg had thought to have the pizza parlor leave some of the toppings off part of the pizza, just in case.

Greg only appeared to be listening, as Maggie rambled on and on.

Lori noticed he was quieter than normal. She cornered Marta and quietly asked, "Everything go okay with you two?"

"Wonderful, almost too wonderful...talk to you later."

This left Lori extremely curious. She decided to say no more and wait until later to talk to Marta, when they were alone.

"Maggie, honey, I must get back to the farm. We'll see you later. You can come back and visit Tinker Bell anytime." She gave a quick wave to Greg and Marta and made her exit.

After Maggie finished her pizza and milk, she went to the sewing room, which no longer surprised them.

Greg suggested he and Marta go to the parlor. They curled up on the sofa together and he began to speak softly, "Mart, it was good. I don't want you to think any differently. It just surprised the heck out of me. I don't know what happened there. I do know that, somehow, it felt right at the moment. It's now that I have questions. Don't get me wrong. I don't question what I felt. I don't actually regret it. But, Mart...how could I? Lisa has only been gone two months, and I have already had sex with another woman—her best friend of all people!"

"Greg, please don't dwell on it. It happened, and it was wonderful! So let it be at that."

They sat quietly for the rest of the evening. Greg turned on the TV, and they became interested in an old Steve Martin movie, Father of the Bride II. They were laughing and enjoying the movie, when Greg surprised Marta by reaching for her hand. Holding hands was a long way from where they were earlier, although it was warm and sweet. It appeared that Greg wouldn't go cold on her now, as she had worried he might.

As Maggie's bedtime approached, they found her still in the sewing room, which was no surprise. Maggie didn't see them standing silently in the doorway listening. "I want to stay in here with you. Daddy doesn't mind if I stay in here. Besides, Johnny needs me." She then began to sing, "Hush, little baby..." Greg turned to Marta. He could see by her expression she was as puzzled as he was.

"Maggie...honey, it's time for bed."

"Oh, Daddy, do I have to?"

"Yes, honey, go on upstairs and get in your jammies. I'll be up in a few minutes to tuck you in."

Maggie reluctantly started toward the front of the house to the spiral staircase. There was no way she was using the back stairway at night.

"What did you make of that?" Marta asked Greg.

"It made no sense at all to me. She must be making believe her mommy is still alive. It concerns me that she hasn't accepted Lisa's death."

"No, that wouldn't be healthy. You need to keep an eye on this," Marta suggested.

"Of course, I will."

Marta decided it was time she head home. It had been a long day, a long, wonderful day. Greg kissed her goodnight and watched her drive away. He was going to miss her after today—that, he knew.

When he got to Maggie's room, he found her tucking her dollies in bed, their day clothes neatly beside them on the window seat. She climbed into bed. He pulled the covers up and sat on the bed beside her. "Maggie, honey, who is Johnny?"

"He's my little baby. I rock him and sing to him. He goes to sleep when I make him happy. I love him. He loves me."

Greg thought that was enough talk for the night. He kissed her goodnight and turned her night light on, as he switched the room light off. This little imaginary friend concerned him, this and the fact she may not have accepted Lisa's death. He put it out of his mind, as he entered his office. He wanted to do some research on hauntings on his computer. As he sat at his desk his mind wandered back to Marta. The day with her really had been quite wonderful. Sex with her was much more than he could have ever expected. He thought about the letter Lisa had left for him. With this thought, he left his office to again read the letter he had returned to her jewelry box. Reading it brought back so much. He carefully read...

You must not grieve for long, honey. Life is too short to spend it in grief. Make Maggie's days happy ones. She has lost her mommy; don't let her lose her daddy to grief. God will be sure to help you. I will help you all I can. Surely, God will give me that much.

In time, you must find someone else to share your life with—a new mommy for Maggie. Yes, honey, I want you to marry again. I know right now this may seem impossible. You will know when the time is right. Please, don't hesitate on my account. There is no set time that you must be alone before you begin to see another. Who cares what people think! I know you love me and will never forget me. This doesn't mean you can't learn to love another. This is what I want for you. You are too young to spend the rest of your life alone—too young and too sexy!

Yes, she definitely was telling him to move on, to

find another love, a new mommy for Maggie. He reread the last few sentences…

There is no set time that you must be alone before you begin to see another. Who cares what people think! I know you love me and will never forget me. This doesn't mean you can't learn to love another. This is what I want for you. You are too young to spend the rest of your life alone—too young and too sexy!

These words began to ring in his mind. *There is no set time. This is what I want for you.* These words, especially, stood out to him.

He undressed and got into bed. He lay there for some time, rethinking the day's events. It was such a full day, from mysteries—to wonderful—to wondering what was happening in Maggie's mind. He rethought what he and Marta had done. He didn't approve. It was way too soon. How could he even think of having sex with Marta—as that was what it was—wasn't it? He loved Lisa and would never forget her. He would always love her. He thought of how he felt with Marta, how warm and loving she was, how much like Lisa she was. Did he forget for a moment that it was Marta, not Lisa? No, he knew it was Marta. And, it didn't seem like just sex. How could it have been anything more? He was puzzled to say the least. It would not happen again—at least not for a long time, regardless of what Lisa wrote. Time did matter. It was far too soon! He wouldn't let himself be so weak.

He finally drifted off. He awoke, or did he? He felt a warm sensation on his penis. The skin was moving. His testicles felt as if they were being touched…or fondled. Then the skin began to move again. This he could see. He began to get an erection, and felt a slight pressure on his thighs. His hard shaft was feeling wonderful. Someone was riding him—hard and deep, faster and faster—harder than he had ever been ridden, too fast, too hard. He felt pain, which was increasing to the point of being unbearable. He began to scream in both pain and terror. The pressure on his thighs lifted. "My God! What has just happened?" Greg was dazed and weak. He began to shake. His legs became like rubber, as he got out of bed and staggered to the shower. When he turned on the shower the water became extremely hot. He frantically turned the knob toward cold. The water only became hotter and hotter. He jumped out of the shower to keep from being scalded. "What the hell was that?" he asked himself. He dried off, put on some shorts and returned to his office. He knew there would be no sleep tonight.

Six

Thanksgiving was a day Greg would rather have forgotten this year. Lori and Steve insisted he and Maggie come to the farm. They promised to keep it simple. Lori had asked Greg if he minded if she was to invite Marta. At first he told her he would rather she didn't; then later he decided it would be okay. He enjoyed Marta's warm nature. She had an easy way of making him laugh.

Lori was anxious to talk to Marta. She had a glow about her that Lori suspected was connected to Greg. She had sensed the night she took Maggie home that there was something different about the two of them.

Greg, Marta, and Maggie all arrived together. Lori was pleased to see how cute they all were together. They arrived laughing and joking, quite unlike how she thought this day would be. The first holiday without Lisa was sure to be a difficult one.

"Here's the salad I made," joked Greg.

"Yeah, you worked really hard making that!" Marta chimed back.

"Thanks, Greg. We really appreciate your hard work," laughed Lori. "Dinner will be ready in about thirty minutes. Have a seat in the living room."

The house smelled delicious. The air was filled with wonderfully delicious turkey and pumpkin pie aromas.

Marta stayed in the kitchen to help Lori.

"Well…" Lori coaxed.

"Well, what?" grinned Marta.

"I think you know what."

"I do?" Marta teased.

"Yes, you do! Out with it! What is that glow you have had since the night I took Maggie home and you were there?"

"I guess it's time I confess. Greg and I were wonderfully close that night."

"Close, as in…"

"Yep!"

"I thought so!" Lori grinned. "It must have been good!"

"Oh, yes, very good!"

"I'm surprised at how soon it happened," Lori said.

"Actually, so am I, and so is Greg. He was a bit troubled about it that night. Somehow, I think he feels okay about it now. We really haven't had a chance to talk about it since that night. I think he was concerned it happened too soon, and he wondered what Lisa would have thought."

Just then Tinker Bell came running into the kitchen. Maggie was trailing her, full of smiles and giggles. "She is soooo cute. I love her to pieces. Don't you think she is just so cute, Marta?"

"She sure is…and frisky, too. I bet she sleeps well."

Lori laughed, "She sure does. After Maggie left last week-end she went to her doggie bed and slept for hours."

*

Greg found this opportunity to talk to Steve alone. "Steve, I don't quite know how to say this…I think our house is haunted."

Steve almost burst out laughing, but he could see how serious Greg was. "What in the world makes you think that?"

"There have been some strange things happening in the house and carriage house for months now, things that I have found no other explanation for. It started before Lisa died. She didn't witness this, and I couldn't tell her, with her being so ill. She had enough to worry about."

"What kind of things?"

"First a red, sticky substance with the stench of death appeared in the loft of the carriage house."

"What was it?" Steve asked.

"I certainly don't know. Then it appeared in the back servants' hallway. I cleaned it up, only to have it reappear. I saw no traces of it for a while, until after Lisa died. It reappeared the night before Marta and I went skiing. Maggie was alone in the house. I had taken a baby monitor receiver out with me so I could hear her. I forgot and left it out there. I went back early the next morning to get it. Much to my surprise, the red substance had disappeared and so had the stench. It makes no sense to me. Then after Marta and I returned home from skiing, she wanted to see the third floor mansard. When I opened the door to the stairway the same stench hit us. There on the steps was the same red substance."

"Wow that *is* very strange. You are saying you

found it at three difference places at different times?"

"Yes and when Marta and I opened the door to go back up to the mansard the next morning it was already back."

"Good Lord, what in the world is going on over there?"

"That's what I would like for you to help me figure out. Until Marta saw it, I hadn't told anyone. I would really appreciate your input on this. Also, there are a few other things. Marta and I brought a painting of a beautiful, young lady down from the mansard and hung it in the spare bedroom at the end of the hall. The next morning, she went in there to look at it again, and it was crying real tears, tears that disappeared after a few minutes. I went to get a broom to sweep up a broken vase that she had knocked over, at the sight of seeing the tears. While I was gone, the tears disappeared. The painting had been wet from the tears; it was now dry. I set the broom beside the stair door. It disappeared. Later it appeared in one of the mansard bedrooms. We hadn't taken it up there."

"Good God, Greg! I would put a lock on that door!"

"Exactly, I did just that the same night." He hesitated a minute. "There's more."

"You've got to be kidding!" Steve said, excitedly.

"I wish I was! This is the eeriest of all."

"You're telling me it gets worse?"

"Oh, yes! That night after Marta left, I got into bed and drifted off to sleep, waking a little later. At least I think I was awake, when I...I was raped. Only, no one was there. No one I could see anyway!"

"Greg, you had to be dreaming!"

"I really don't think I was, Steve. I knew I wasn't

when I found I was in dire need of a shower. I was a mess. I stepped into the shower and about got scalded. I turned the knob to cold and the water only got hotter and hotter. I had to jump out to keep from getting burned. That water was hotter than I have ever felt it. The next morning I tested the water to see if it ever got that hot. I ran it for quite some time. It never got anywhere close to being that hot."

"This is strange."

"I'll say," replied Greg. Ready to hear more?"

"There's more?"

"Yes, before Lisa ever got sick, we both heard a baby crying. Maggie made the comment she had a dream in which a baby was crying. Lisa and I heard it different times. For a while after her death, I didn't hear it. I heard it again the night the red substance first appeared on the mansard stairway. Now tell me this house isn't haunted."

"I sure wish I could. I have no idea what is going on in that house of yours. Mind if I come over some time and check things out? Or...better yet, if this red substance should appear again give me a call. I'll rush over and see it for myself."

"Okay, be prepared to be spooked. It's the spookiest thing I have ever seen. Well...before the invisible rapist anyway. Actually one previous night, I may also have been raped. It was entirely different though. This was gentle and loving. The other night was far from gentle. I've never been ridden so hard before. It was as if someone wanted to hurt me."

"Be sure and call if that happens again. Maybe I can get in on some of the fun," Steve laughed.

"It's not funny, Steve."

"I know, sorry, it's just that it's so unbelievable I

can't help but laugh."

"You don't believe me then?" Greg was a bit irritated.

"No, it isn't that. I believe you. You couldn't possibly make up a story so wild."

Just then Maggie and Tinker Bell came running in, "I'm supposed to tell you dinner is ready!"

"Sure smells good!" Greg was glad for a diversion.

"Oh, would you look at that bird," Steve was admiring the beautiful, golden brown turkey. "Looks like we have enough to feed an army."

Lori smiled, "Sometimes you two eat like you were in the army and had been in battle for weeks with nothing to eat except army rations!"

After they were seated Steve said the blessing. "Dear Lord, thank you for all this wonderful food and all our blessings. And Lord…take good care of Lisa."

This took Greg and the others off guard. Greg wiped tears away. Steve wondered if it had been a mistake to mention Lisa. He began carving the turkey and dishing out portions, as he passed the plates down. The other dishes were then passed, as they began the meal in silence, all thinking of Lisa.

Maggie broke the silence. "Does Tinker Bell get some?"

"We'll see to her later," chuckled Lori.

The day went well—much better than any of them thought it would, although Lisa's absence was obvious. Having Marta there and the new little puppy seemed to help. Greg said no more to Steve about the mysterious happenings, as they weren't alone much. Maggie was in and out with the puppy. It was good to see her having so much fun. Her smiles and giggles were good for all.

Greg, Marta, and Maggie left early evening. After

the short drive home, Maggie again went to the sewing room where she sat in the rocking chair, giggling, reading, and singing. Marta, puzzled, stood out of Maggie's sight and watched her for some time. How could she be so happy, never seeming to miss her mommy? They had been so close. Greg had no answers either. It was difficult to understand. As long as she was happy there seemed to be no need for a counselor.

After they tucked Maggie into bed, they walked down the hall toward the sitting room to make sure all looked okay. Greg pulled on the padlock to make sure it was locked tightly. It didn't budge. Marta wanted to go through more of the old boxes up in the mansard, but they both thought it was best not to go up there after dark, especially with Maggie in the house. They went into the guest room to take a peek at the newly hung picture. It was fine—no tears. It did rather dampen the feeling one used to have when entering the room.

They walked down the back staircase, knowing the baby monitor was on in Maggie's room with the receiver in the parlor. They sat on the sofa in front of the fireplace talking about this, that, and everything. Again Marta expressed her desire to search through more boxes on the third floor. Greg agreed to her coming over the next morning. Maggie was to spend the day with one of her little friends while on Thanksgiving break from school.

Greg had intended to slow things down with Marta. He still felt the timing of what happened was not good. As they sat close with his arm around her, his hormones began to think differently. Once his lips met hers the fire was lit. There was no stopping for either of them. They had already had a taste of the forbidden fruit. Quickly they undressed one another, leaving only their sexy underwear. He cupped his hand between her thighs. Thoughts and feelings raced. Their under garments, which had been tossed in the air, were soon hanging from the furniture. His passionate tongue and clever fingers drove her up another notch. She thrust herself toward him, almost out of control. She grabbed his hard shaft begging—shocking Greg, as he hadn't known this side of her. As he thrust himself deep inside her, she gasped, following with quiet moans. Seeing her like this was such a turn on for him. Things became quite intense—perhaps wild. Greg was quickly learning to like this wild side of Marta, although it didn't last long. They lay in the arms of one another, not caring what the rest of the world would think, if they knew.

This is slowing things down? Greg thought to himself. He didn't approve, but oh, how he enjoyed!

Eventually, they dozed off.

They were awakened by the cry of a baby that seemed to be coming through the baby monitor. Greg hurriedly put on his shorts, grabbed the receiver, and ran upstairs to Maggie's room. By the time he got to the head of the stairs, the cries had stopped. Of course there was no baby to be seen. There never was. In fact, everything looked quite normal upstairs. Maggie was sound asleep. Greg started down the spiral staircase and met Marta half way down. By now, she was fully dressed, much to Greg's disappointment.

"Marta, let's go back to the parlor," he whispered.

He threw some pillows on the floor in front of the fireplace, stretched out, and invited Marta to join him. As she lay in his arms, it suddenly occurred to him, "Marta, I never stopped to think when we put Maggie to bed, that I wouldn't be able to take you home. I picked you up this morning, remember?"

"I wasn't thinking either."

"You know, with Maggie in the house, we have to be careful...morals, you know."

"I agree, Greg. We don't want Maggie growing up thinking it's okay to sleep with someone before marriage. Besides that, how could we expect her to understand what we are doing, when we don't understand it ourselves?"

He drew her closer. "Marta, I think Lisa understands...if I could just get myself to understand. I hadn't planned on this happening again tonight. Once I got close to you, I couldn't help myself. Lisa left a letter for me to read after she died. In it, she told me to move on. She told me not to grieve for long, as life is too short. She also told me there is no set time that I must be alone before I begin to see another. She didn't want me to worry about what others think. So, I have decided not to think about others and what they might think. This is between you, me, and Maggie." He then gave her a sweet gentle kiss. "Marta, do you really want to sleep in all those clothes? Is it okay with you if we sleep down here, or would you rather sleep in the guest room?"

"I hope you are joking! No way am I sleeping in that room with the crying picture. No way!"

"Maybe we should retire that portrait to the mansard. What do you think?" Greg asked.

"Well, are you trying to get out of sleeping beside me the next time I stay? This is where I would choose regardless of where the picture was." She snuggled up closer to Greg.

"I really hate to move an inch now, but the hall closet has a blanket and some bed pillows. I'll be right back."

For a second Greg thought he saw a flash of light moving toward the kitchen at the other end of the hall. He convinced himself it was a reflection of some sort from a streetlight outside the window.

When he returned to Marta, she was in her bra and panties. How gorgeous she looked, lying there on her back in a deep purple satin bra and matching bikini panties. He lay down beside her, placed the blanket over them, and put his arm around her. She kissed him. He returned the kiss and desires again arose. They were soon rolling on the floor kissing, touching, tasting, and...making love?

They slept skin-to-skin until early morning when Greg awoke. "Marta sweetie, it's time to wake up and get some clothes on before Maggie wakes up. Would you like to shower?"

"That would be nice, but I hate to put the same clothes back on. They are a little too dressy for going to the third floor to scrounge around."

"Lisa's clothes are still upstairs. You are close to her size. I'm sure you can find some jeans and a sweatshirt or something. Would you mind wearing her clothes? I know Lisa would love for you to."

"If you're sure it's okay. It will seem a little strange, although I do need some different clothes."

Greg escorted her upstairs and waited his turn in the bedroom, while she showered. He heard her let out a scream, as she jumped out of the shower and into the bedroom. "That water almost scalded me! I kept turning it to colder, and it kept getting hotter."

"Oh, Marta, I'm so sorry. "Are you okay?"

"I think so. Do you see any burns on me?"

"Well, ah...I don't think so. Turn around and let

me see." She turned a 360. "I think you are okay, but…" He reached over and put his hand between her legs, at the y. "Does this feel burned?"

"Greg! Shame on you!" she teased, as she slapped his hand away.

"Go dry off and find some clothes before it's too late."

Marta grabbed a towel and proceeded to dry herself off while Greg checked the shower out. The water seemed fine. He threw his shorts at Marta and jumped in. He could hear her laughter as he got under the shower and lathered up. Just as he was ready to rinse off the water began getting extremely hot. Greg stuck with it, convinced there was nothing wrong with it. He quickly became sure he was wrong. He, too, had to jump out, almost knocking Marta off her feet.

"Greg, you are red as a beet! You look like you might be burned. You need to get some lotion on your skin to cool it down. Do you have any aloe vera lotion?"

Greg reached into the medicine cabinet. "Right here, baby."

"Go lie on the bed, and I'll rub it on you."

"You sure that's safe, sweetie?"

Marta pulled the spread and covers back, so she wouldn't get lotion on them. Greg lay down. Marta, still nude, began to rub the lotion on his body. She momentarily stopped, walked over to the door, closed it tightly, and locked it so Maggie wouldn't walk in if she woke up.

"Good idea, hon." Greg's eyes were on her fabulous body as she walked to the bedroom door and back to him.

Marta again squeezed some lotion onto her hand

and began applying it to Greg's handsome, muscular body. She hadn't taken such notice before; now that she had him totally naked lying there in front of her, she was noticing he was much more muscular than she had ever known. She smiled at the thought that she probably was always too horny to notice before. She loved his broad shoulders and his handsomely developed pectoral muscles. He worked out often at the gym the law firm provided for the employees. His chest was moderately hairy; this, to her, was quite sexy. As she rubbed the lotion in, the once curly brown hairs succumbed to the lotion.

"Can you spread your legs for me?" Marta asked.

"Can I? Gladly sweetie. Sounds like something I might ask of you," he chuckled.

She rubbed some lotion on his tight, partially hairy, thighs and continued on down to his feet. She pretended not to notice his manhood was thickening, although she, too, was beginning to have desires. Greg already knew that, as when she got up to lock the door, he noticed her nipples had begun to respond.

Eventually, desires took over. She climbed on and began to ride him. He was so slick with lotion it was difficult to stay on his hips. She leaned forward, greasing her breasts with lotion, as her exuberant breasts slapped against his chest. Their lips met, in a moist, intimate kiss. Their bond was growing much stronger. She sat up straight and rode him hard, until they were moaning—quietly, so Maggie wouldn't hear. Marta fell limp against his slick body. Together, they began to laugh. She now had more lotion on her than he did. They got up and began wiping each other off with towels, laughing, knowing it wouldn't take much to wind up back in bed.

They became more serious when Greg opened a drawer and showed Marta where to find Lisa's clothes. This had broken the mood. Marta chose some appropriate clothes and put them on. She wore her own bra, as Lisa's was a smaller cup. She didn't feel right about wearing Lisa's panties, but she wanted to smell clean.

Greg dressed in blue jeans and a sweatshirt and started toward Maggie's bedroom to check on her. Marta stopped him long enough to give him a gentle kiss. "Thanks Greg, for everything." He smiled and went on to check on Maggie. Actually, he needed a moment to pull himself together after seeing Marta in Lisa's clothes. Maggie was still fast asleep. He and Marta went down the back stairs to the kitchen to start breakfast.

"I really must get a plumber to check on that shower. It happened to me last week, too. I checked it out and couldn't find anything wrong. It had been fine since then. Now, I'll have someone come look at it. You must admit, some good did come out of the problem today." He smiled at Marta and began making coffee. "So, what would you like for breakfast? Omelet or waffles?"

"Omelet sounds good to me. What kind do you make?"

"Usually bacon and cheese. I can add green pepper and onion too, if you would like. I have found many short cuts, frozen foods and bacon already prepared, even bacon bits in a pinch."

"Sounds like you are becoming quite the chef since…" Her voice trailed off, not wanting to mention Lisa's name. "Bacon and cheese sounds fine to me."

Maggie came down all dressed, as Greg was

dishing up the omelets, which looked more like scrambled eggs to Marta. She kept quiet on this one. Greg really was doing well.

"I took a shower, exclaimed Maggie. I hope it's okay with you that I used your shower. I love that fancy room.

Greg and Marta's mouths both dropped open. "Did that go okay?" Greg asked.

"Sure, I think I got clean."

"Was the water warm enough?" Greg asked so as not to scare her.

"It was okay. It was a little cool. Who used up all the hot water, anyway?"

"Marta spent the night, and we both had showers this morning."

"Oh?" Maggie looked puzzled.

Greg hadn't stopped to think Maggie might use the master bath shower this morning without saying anything. She ordinarily used the main bath.

"So you are all nice and clean now to go with your little friend."

"Daddy, did you forget again? Her name is Kaitlyn."

"No, honey. I didn't forget again. I was just teasing you."

As Greg and Marta were doing the dishes, Kaitlyn and her mom came to the door. Maggie was in the sewing room. Marta went to tell her they were there. She heard Maggie say, "Bye, bye, be back soon."

Marta wondered who she was telling good-bye. More than likely, it was an imaginary friend. Maggie kissed Greg good-bye and was out the door in a flash. Marta wondered if it was her imagination, or had she gotten a strange look from Kaitlyn's mom? She refused to let it bother her.

"Greg, are you ready for our fun in the mansard now?" Marta asked.

"Fun? I don't know if I would classify opening that stair door fun, after what we have seen!"

"I know. I feel the same way. It does scare me some. I refuse to let it keep me out of the mansard. There are too many old treasures up there to let them stay there and rot without us enjoying them."

"You win, I guess." Greg put the last dish in the cupboard and turned to give Marta a kiss. "I love those soft, sweet lips of yours. Let's go."

*

Greg took the key from his pocket and unlocked the new lock. The door was open only a crack when the stench hit them. "God, no! Not again! I'm calling Steve!" The dreaded red stuff was back, covering more of the stairs than before. He slammed the door shut and locked it. He and Marta went downstairs to the parlor to make the call to Steve.

"I'll be there in a flash," Steve told Greg.

And he was! Greg couldn't believe how quickly he got there—a large flashlight in hand.

"Lead the way! This I have got to see!" Steve requested.

They led him up the back stairway. Greg quickly turned the key in the lock and opened the door.

Steve jumped back. "God—the smell! It smells like rotten bodies!"

"Yes, it's quite bad, isn't it?" Greg agreed.

Steve stepped forward for a look. There on the stairs was the blood-like substance dripping down the stairs in massive amounts. He ran his finger across it and rubbed them together. "Feels like blood."

"Yes, I know it does, so much like it that it's eerie," Greg commented.

"What the hell do you suppose it is?" Steve asked.

"That's what you are supposed to be helping me figure out!" Greg exclaimed.

"You say this same stuff was in the back hall and in the carriage house?"

"It sure was."

"How long since you have checked out there?" Steve asked.

"It's been awhile. I've been leaving my Tahoe out, so I don't have to go in there. It's far too eerie to go in there every time I need to use the Tahoe."

"Let's go out there now. I want to see if the stuff has come back," Steve suggested.

"Okay…for you, I will do it. It won't be so bad in the daylight. Not so sure I would be so agreeable after dark. That carriage house has a feel about it, even without the red substance. I may have to tear it down. I really hate to do that, as Lisa loved it so. She thought it suited the house. She never knew about the damn red stuff!"

Marta didn't want to go with the guys. Then again, there was no way she wanted to stay in the house by herself, so she followed. A chill came over her as they neared the carriage house. Little did she know that Greg also felt the eeriness. He had learned to hate this building. As he unlatched the door, he knew by the stench the substance was back. He pulled the door open to find the red substance was now in the carriage room, which he used as a garage. Steve's mouth dropped open. Greg slammed the door shut. Marta clung to him tightly.

"There is a back door. Let's go around to the old stable and see if we can get in that way without walking through this shit," Greg said in disgust. The others followed, standing back as Greg opened the door, "Jesus Christ, it's everywhere!"

Steve was certainly getting his chance to view the crimson substance. Marta clung tighter to Greg. She was shaking inside, hoping it didn't show. There wasn't a spot on the floor that wasn't covered. The trap door was closed, with massive amounts oozing through the cracks. They could well see that the entire carriage house was taken over by the red stuff.

"Just let it rot in the stuff!" Greg motioned for the others to move back, slammed the door, and started walking toward the house—when the sky darkened. Thunder clapped. It began to look like midnight, instead of morning. Horrendous lightning was flashing everywhere, like none they had ever seen. They ran to the house, as frightened as three small children about to be captured by a monster in a horror film.

No one spoke for twenty minutes, while they sat at the kitchen table. Steve began to look puzzled, "Notice anything strange about this storm?"

Greg thought for a bit, "It certainly is severe. Is that what you mean?"

"No, there is not a drop of rain. Besides that…this is late November. It's too cold for a thunderstorm," Steve explained.

"This is certainly something to think about. Perhaps this is one to be added to the list of mysteries," Greg replied.

"With all these mysteries, has anyone really been hurt?" Steve asked.

"Well, almost getting scalded wasn't very pleasant...and getting raped downright hurt."

"What did you just say, Greg? Did you say you were raped?" Marta asked, in disbelief.

"Oh sweetie, I didn't mean to blurt that out. We do need to talk."

Steve quickly dismissed himself, "While you two talk, I will go up and take a look at the mansard stairs." Greg took the keys from his pants pocket and handed them to Steve.

Greg hugged Marta and led her to the parlor. She sat extremely close to Greg. He put his arm around her and began to tell her the whole story. Marta was amazed at what he had to say. He concluded by telling her he didn't know what happened; although he was sure he was not asleep. This combined with the scalding water made him very uneasy, but he didn't want Marta to know he was connecting the two.

"No change upstairs. I locked the door when I left," Steve said, as he handed Greg the keys.

"So, what do you make of it all, Steve?" Greg asked, keeping Marta close.

"I certainly don't know what to make of it. This is the strangest thing I have ever encountered. It does appear to be on the side of hauntings."

This made a chill run through Marta, even though she herself had felt this to be the case. She and Greg both could find no other explanation.

Steve sat for a while, deep in thought. "Have you tried searching the Internet for anything like this?"

Greg looked at Marta, then, back at Steve, "Yes, Marta and I both have searched the net. There are many sites on haunting. None mention anything of a red, sticky substance...none that we have found yet.

We'll continue searching."

"I plan to go to the library and see what I can find there," Marta was still totally thrown by the rape Greg had just explained to her.

"I guess there's nothing more I can do here. I should get back to Lori. I left her wondering what was going on over here, since you didn't give much of an explanation over the phone."

*

After Steve left, Greg and Marta sat quietly in the parlor. Each was deep in thought. Marta felt safe for now, while she was in Greg's arms, where she most enjoyed being. It was still difficult for her to believe they had become so close, so soon after Lisa's death. Each was grieving Lisa. Each needed someone. Since they were both grieving the same person, it seemed only natural that they spend time together. The time they spent with one another seemed to be drawing them closer and closer. It wasn't just the time together; it was partially due to the strange occurrences in the house.

Marta finally broke the silence. "I think we should return the portrait to the mansard. It's also a mystery of this house. It no longer seems beautiful to me. It needs to be removed from the living quarters, if not from this house."

"When do you suggest we do this?"

"No better time than right now."

"How do you propose we get beyond the beloved red substance?"

"We walk right through it! That stuff isn't real—it's fake. I don't pretend to understand how it gets here. It's not blood, or it wouldn't have disappeared by itself that time. It's obviously meant to scare us, and I'm not going to let it scare me any longer. This is a beautiful home that should be enjoyed."

"Then, why are you so scared of the portrait?" Greg grinned.

"Well... well... I'm not scared of it! I just don't like it anymore. It doesn't compliment the guest room. That should be a happy room for guests, not a room that sheds tears!"

Her comments amused Greg, as he knew that painting spooked her. "Okay, if you insist, we will go upstairs and walk right through that nice red stuff!"

Greg unlocked the mansard door. Marta stood behind him, trembling, pretending not to be afraid. Neither noticed the familiar stench as Greg opened the door. Marta peeked around him. Much to her surprise she saw no red substance.

"Oh, my God, how in the world!" Greg exclaimed.

"Yes, how in the world did it leave so fast? Steve was just up here and said nothing had changed—the red stuff was still here. See, I told you the stuff was fake, and that it was nothing to get all scared about!" Marta pretended to never have been afraid.

"Let's get the portrait and take it upstairs, while we have the all clear here," Greg suggested.

Marta suddenly became brave and ran into the guest room, quickly grabbed the portrait off the wall, and ran back and handed it to Greg.

"This old picture looks like there were never any tears shed. It's a shame to have to put her back in storage." Even with all the spookiness, Greg was enjoying teasing Marta.

"Greg, she's got to go! Get moving upward. I'll be

right behind you." Marta really was in a hurry to dispose of this lovely lady. Greg stuffed it in a box and they were back downstairs in a flash. Greg was ready to walk down the hall to the parlor, when Marta spoke up. "Let's go out to the carriage house and check on the red stuff out there."

"Marta, haven't you had enough for one day? I want to forget all this and sit and enjoy each other."

"We can do that later," Marta insisted.

This time it was Greg trembling, as they neared the carriage house. After all, he was the one who first discovered the red, sticky substance. Being alone had made it all the spookier. Memories of that night, not so long ago, were still quite vivid. It had scared the shit out of him. Nevertheless, he had let Marta talk him into coming back out to check it. He lifted the latch and slowly opened the door to find the red stuff was totally gone. The floor was clean.

Seven

"There ain't nothin' wrong with this shower, Mr. Greg. I've checked it from top to bottom. It's as fit as a fiddle." Hank turned and looked at Greg, wondering why he even called him.

"Okay, Hank. I just wanted to make sure. I didn't want anyone getting burned."

"Ain't nobody gonna get burned in this shower, unless they turn the knob to all hot. Want me to turn the water temp down a bit, Mr. Greg?"

"That might not be a bad idea." Greg told him where to find the water heater. He was back upstairs in a few short minutes. Greg paid him, and he was on his way. Greg really didn't know what to think. Maybe Hank wasn't the best man for something like this. He wasn't a licensed plumber—a jack-of-all-trades was more like it.

Greg had promised Maggie they would get the Christmas tree today. It had always been a fun family day to go to a nearby tree forest and cut their own. This year would not be the same without Lisa. She had always especially loved this day. Greg had thought of asking Marta to go along. He had decided it should be a day for him and Maggie alone, as they were now the family. Marta would come to the house later and help decorate the tree, which would be placed in the grand drawing room. This room was the most appropriate room for a large tree, as the ceilings were thirteen feet high. He and Lisa had loved the beautiful trees they had cut in previous years, although they had wished they could be larger. They had dreamed of the time when they would have a home large enough for a huge blue spruce.

Lisa had always insisted they look at each and every tree, before coming back to the original find. By this time, Greg was ready to cut any one she chose. In earlier years, they pulled Maggie on a sled, as the tree farm was quite large. Now, she had more energy than Greg.

As they pulled into the tree farm, Maggie hopped out of the Tahoe before Greg could get his seat belt off. She was all smiles and full of giggles. As they walked the tree farm, they kept their eyes open for that perfect tree. Maggie saw many trees, which she thought was that special one. Greg nicely convinced her that special tree was still out there. Maggie's special tree could be scraggly or totally bare on one side. To her, they all looked great. After they had covered almost the entire forest, they came upon that special one. And yes, it was close to their starting point. It was a beautiful blue spruce, somewhat taller than thirteen feet. Greg knew Lisa would be pleased with their choice. As usual, they would need to cut some off. They always used the extra greens for decorating the house. Greg told Maggie to stand back while he cut it down. Just as it was ready to fall, Maggie stepped closer to look at a pinecone inside the tree. Greg looked up to see she had stepped into the path of the falling tree. He yelled for her to get back. Just then, he saw a golden glow appear behind her. At that very moment, it looked as if she had been grabbed from behind and pulled out of the way. The tree crashed to the ground in the very spot where Maggie had been standing. She appeared dazed.

"Maggie, honey, are you okay?" Greg asked, as he rushed to her.

"Yes, Daddy, I'm fine." She looked behind her, scanning the tree forest, as if looking for something. "Daddy, somebody grabbed me. They pulled me back. Who was it, Daddy?"

"Maybe it was your guardian angel. Suppose?"

"Really, do you think so? Are there really guardian angels?"

"I believe so, sweetheart. I have always heard they protect us." Greg was anxious to tell Marta about this.

A young man, who worked for the tree farm, pulled the tree to the parking area with a garden tractor and loaded it onto the wagon Greg had attached to the Tahoe.

Greg thought about the angel incident all the way home. Could it have been Lisa? He felt Lisa had been there with them, just as she was probably with them many times since her death.

A light snow was beginning to fall as they entered the driveway. "It's the perfect touch for the spirit of Christmas, isn't it sweetheart? Mommy would have loved this."

"Yes, she will, Daddy."

Greg untied the tree and took it up onto the side porch, where he already had the tree stand waiting. He had known this tree would need a sturdier stand than the one they had always used. This one would definitely require the homemade stand.

Before long, Greg had the tree cut to length and in the stand, with many greens leftover to use for decorating. Maggie had watched with much enthusiasm and chatter. Her enthusiasm easily rubbed off onto Greg. She was such a bubbly, adorable child. Greg explained to her they must carry it around to the front door, instead of dragging it through the whole house. He grabbed the tree by the stand and Maggie quickly latched onto the top of the tree, happily feeling she was a big help, as she sang "Oh, Christmas tree, oh, Christmas tree, of all the trees most lovely." She would repeat the same line, hum a few bars, and repeat what she had just sung. She obviously didn't know the rest of the words. Just as they had the tree in place in the grand drawing room, the doorbell rang at the back of the house. Greg hurried to the door. There stood Marta weighted down with many packages.

"What in the heck do you have there?" he asked as he took the packages from her.

"Ornaments for that blue spruce, what else? Oops, you did get a blue spruce didn't you?"

"Of course, we all knew that was what Lisa had dreamed of for this year," Greg replied.

They found Maggie still in the grand drawing room, admiring the tree. "Isn't it beautiful, Marta?"

"Oh, yes, it's perfect!" Marta began opening the packages and showing Maggie the new ornaments. She oohed and aahed at each one.

"Leave it to you to think of this, Marta. This tree is far too large for the few ornaments we have."

"Greg, last year when Lisa and I were shopping we looked at ornaments just like these. Lisa was dreaming of the day she would buy these for the perfect blue spruce." Greg smiled affectionately at Marta, for he should have known she would know exactly what Lisa would have wanted.

Greg strung the lights. Yes, Marta had also bought more lights. She had remembered exactly the type of lights Greg and Lisa had on the tree the year before. Maggie waited impatiently for him to finish stringing the lights so she could hang the ornaments. Lisa had taught her not to clump too many of the same kind together. Many of the old ornaments had special meaning. They brought back memories of previous Christmases. Baby's first Christmas had always been there for Maggie, and the rocking horse, the crystal teddy bears, Rudolf, the Santa with his fat tummy, and many more. It was late by the time the tree was decorated.

"Maggie, honey, time for bed." Greg knew she would fight him, as she was still wound up from the adventures of the day.

"Daddy, I am wide awake. There is something I need to do first." She ran down the hall and disappeared into the parlor.

Marta knew she was again going to the sewing room. "Is she still spending as much time in there as she was?"

"Oh, yes. Nothing has changed. I keep thinking she will eventually spend less and less time in there. I tell myself to be happy she isn't sad and crying all the time with Lisa gone. Then I wonder if this is healthy. I have an idea that I hope will help. You know how she loves little Tinker Bell."

"Oh, yes! She definitely has a bond with that little pup," Marta agreed.

"Lori tells me the lady that owns the kennel, where she got Tinker Bell, has a litter of Yorkshire terriers, soon to be ready for adoption. Lori and I were discussing this Maggie situation, her obsession with the sewing room and the rocking chair. We wonder if it would help if she had a puppy of her own."

"You know, Greg, I think this could be the answer for Maggie."

"I was thinking of surprising her with the puppy for Christmas."

Greg drew Marta close and kissed her. Looking into her eyes he said, "Hi, sweetie. I have missed you." She smiled back, as if to say she had missed him, too.

"Want to spend the night? You can sleep upstairs with me. We must get up earlier than Maggie, though. That shouldn't be a problem, as she is such a sleepy head."

"My bag is in the car. I will be right back."

"You little devil you! You planned to stay all along!"

"Only if you asked!" she laughed.

"I'll get it for you. It's getting dark. I don't like to be out there in the dark myself. Not with all this weird stuff going on around here. You stay here. I'll take the boxes to the back hall storage and then grab your bag on the way back."

"It's in the back seat," Marta yelled as he was half way down the hall.

When Greg neared the kitchen he saw a streak of light. It seemed to come from nowhere and disappear into nowhere, about as quickly as it had come. *I don't know about this house,* he thought to himself, *babies crying in the night, the red substance that seems to come and go, the uncontrollable hot water, crying portraits, streaks of light—what next?* He was seriously considering selling Lisa's dream—their dream.

As Marta waited near the Christmas tree, she wondered which was worse—the creepy darkness outside, or all the mysterious happenings inside.

"Brrr, winter is definitely setting in. Is this the bag?" Greg asked, as he brushed the snow off his shirtsleeves and handed Marta a red floral bag.

"None other."

"I guess I'd better go get Maggie. It's past her bedtime," Greg said.

Marta followed him to the sewing room. They stood in the doorway and watched, as she quietly sang a little tune while she rocked. Neither was sure what the tune was, as it was a new one to them. Her little eyelids kept closing. Each time they closed, she stopped singing. They would open again and a few more words would come out, until her eyes again closed and the singing would stop, as before. Greg picked her up and carried her upstairs. Marta dropped her bag at the master bedroom door and followed Greg into Maggie's room. She helped her get into a little nightgown, which Lisa had made for her a few weeks before her death. Greg pulled the covers up, and they both kissed her good night. Marta paused at the door to look back at Maggie. "She is so sweet, so precious," she whispered to Greg.

*

It had been awhile since Greg and Marta had been alone. He wanted her, but he was still fighting his desires. "How about some eggnog?"

"Sure, sounds good to me," Marta had thought he would whisk her off to the bedroom as soon as Maggie was asleep. Instead, he was leading her to the kitchen.

He opened the refrigerator, took out a carton of eggnog, poured two glasses, and sat them on the table. "Mart, how do you feel about what is happening between us now that you have had a chance to think it over for a while?"

"Maybe I should ask you that? How do you feel about it?"

"Not fair, I asked you first."

"Greg, it's no secret how I have felt about you for a long time. This makes it a little different for me. Of course, I feel a little like I'm taking over what is Lisa's, but she's gone, and we can never bring her back. And there is her wish...her letter to you. I think at this point we should let happen whatever happens and go from there."

"Mart, sweetie, I was hoping you would feel this way. What has happened between us has seemed so good. I'm not prepared to go backward. If it wasn't Lisa's wish, I would do just that, though. Since it's her choice, I want to be with you and let happen whatever will." He got up from the table and put his arms around her, "Sweetie, I have missed you. I just needed some time to think this through, and, also, to give you time to think."

They held each other closely. Greg pressed his body so close she could feel his hard flesh against her. She picked up the empty eggnog glasses and placed them in the sink. He came up behind her, brushing his thickened flesh against her as she stood at the sink. Since she already had desires, this instantly lit a fire within her. She arched her back to meet him. He slowly lowered her slacks, teasing, testing her, and then slid her panties down her shapely thighs. He reached under, placing his hand on her love nest, feeling her wetness.

His fingers lingered and desires rose higher. Her heart began beating faster with the sound of his zipper. As he parted her and his flesh entered, her breathing intensified…she was now all his. The next minutes were unbelievably wild, taking them to their peak quite rapidly. When they came down, he spun her around to hold her, to kiss her, to welcome her back into his arms and into his life. "Sweetie, I shouldn't have done that. I don't know what got into me. I'm sorry. I know it must have seemed animal like. You mean much more to me than that.

"Greg, honey, it's okay. I enjoyed it. You must have noticed it gave me a bit of a rush. It was a long wait until we were alone. I do hope you locked the door though. We wouldn't have wanted anyone walking in on us."

Greg hadn't locked the door, but he didn't tell Marta that. He just smiled. He knew she had enjoyed it. That didn't make him feel any better about how he had handled it. He wanted to treat her as a lady, not as he had just done.

He wandered off to lock the door before they went up to bed. Much to his surprise, the door was locked. This puzzled him, as he knew he had not locked it, and he was sure Marta hadn't. She hadn't known what he had planned.

He returned to the kitchen and led Marta upstairs to his bed, where they snuggled and talked until they drifted off.

Greg awoke first and looked at the clock. He kissed Marta softly, "Sweetie, it's time to get up. We certainly don't want Maggie to find us."

"I need to shower. You did say you had the shower fixed, didn't you?" Marta inquired.

"Yes, Hank came yesterday. He said it's fine. Care if I join you?" he asked with that sexy smile of his. Marta returned his smile. Greg turned the shower on and tested the water before allowing Marta to get in. Together, they stepped in. He began lathering her back with a scented soap he had bought for her. He worked his way around to her breasts, then down to her thighs. Marta knew he was teasing. She wished they had more time. He reached between her thighs as she spread and let him in. Gently, he lathered and washed, much more thoroughly than was necessary. He wanted her badly; there was no time. His fingers were a bit playful.

"Mmm," she smiled, contentedly.

Greg knew if he went any further, it would be too late. "Your turn," he handed Marta a bar of manly deodorant soap. She started with his manhood, which was begging for attention, lathering and massaging all that desired her attention. Next, she washed his back and worked her way down his legs and back up again on the front of his legs, skipping over the parts she had already washed. Now she was teasing! She gently sucked his nipples before washing his chest. Oh, how his sexy, masculine body turned her on. How could they not please each other now?

They stepped under the shower spray to rinse off, side by side, first facing the water, and then turning to rinse their backs. The water suddenly became scalding hot. They jumped out together as the room was filling with steam. Greg closed the door behind them, leaving the water on. "Are you okay, sweetie?"

"Fine, I think, just a bit shaken. I thought Hank said it was fine!"

"Actually, he said he didn't find anything wrong with it. I'll run down to the other bath and get some towels. Be right back!"

When he returned, he handed Marta a soft white towel, and they quickly dried themselves off. The heat of the moment had definitely passed.

Marta reached into her bag and took out a bright green bra and bikini panties to match. Greg watched as she put them on. "I see you are dressing for the season." He reached into his drawer and pulled out some skimpy, red briefs Lisa had given him for Valentine's Day one year.

Marta laughed, "Okay, so now we are a matching Christmas set."

They finished dressing. Maggie could be heard stirring, as they passed her room on their way to the front stairs, to again look at the beautiful tree. They both gasped at the same precise moment. The tree was covered with the red substance and dripping from the lower branches onto the hardwood floor. The stench was overwhelming. Even so, they stood frozen looking at the tree that had been so magnificent the night before. How would they keep Maggie from seeing this?

They ran back up the steps to find Maggie shivering, wrapped in a towel. "Who used all the hot water again?"

Greg explained to her that there had been a problem in the master bath. "Breakfast will be ready in a few minutes. We're having pancakes with strawberries and whipped cream," Greg hoped his quick menu change would divert her attention from the tree, for a few minutes, anyway.

"Mmm, yummy!" She momentarily forgot about the tree and followed Greg and Marta down the hall to the back stairs.

Greg was glad he had bought strawberries and an

aerosol can of whipping cream. These and a bottle of premixed pancakes definitely were coming in handy today. Maggie set the table as Marta took the strawberries from the refrigerator, and Greg heated up the griddle. Within minutes, breakfast was ready. Maggie gobbled down her pancakes and quickly drank her milk. She took off down the hall toward the grand drawing room before they could stop her. Their hearts sank.

As they got to the end of the hall, they could see Maggie standing facing the tree, her mouth wide open, and her eyes glaring toward the tree.

"Isn't it beautiful?"

Amazingly, the red substance was gone. The tree was every bit as beautiful as it was the night before. Marta and Greg could not believe their eyes. The red substance had again vanished as quickly as it had appeared.

*

The Christmas season was difficult for Greg. There were so many memories of Lisa. She had been gone long enough now that it seemed as if she should be coming home from wherever she had gone. Her death was beginning to be more of a reality than in the previous months. As he was shopping at the mall one day, he walked past Victoria Secrets. Tears welled up in his eyes remembering the sexy lingerie he had purchased for her—his beautiful, sweet Lisa. He felt guilty for the times he had been intimate with Marta. He knew it wasn't right, as he still loved Lisa. What was it with Marta? Was it just sex? He enjoyed her company too much for it to be only sex. Was it that he was lonesome, and she helped fill the hours? He knew it was more than that. Could he possibly love her and Lisa at the same time?

Greg had hired a licensed plumber to check the shower. It again checked out okay. Greg no longer trusted it. He was showering in the main bath now. The house was beginning to seem eerier. There were now more streaks of light about the house. His thoughts went more and more toward selling. He would put off the decision until after Christmas. He knew he couldn't go on like this, although it would be hard to give up Lisa's dream. Sleep was a problem for him. He wasn't handling the issue of Maggie's dependence on the sewing room well. It was time to get help, unless a new puppy would be the answer.

He had phoned Marta, but had not seen her since they decorated the tree. She had stayed all that next day helping decorate the mantels. Even her taste in decorating was much like Lisa's. She had done a beautiful job on the mantels.

Two weeks had passed. Greg was having trouble with his shopping. In the past, Lisa had done most of it. He had no idea what to buy Maggie, other than the puppy. He called Marta to see if she would help out. Of course, she had accepted. They decided to get a preview of the puppy before shopping.

Greg found himself quite anxious to see Marta. It seemed much longer than two weeks. Yes, it definitely was more than sex. She was forever full of energy, a bubbly gal, always making him smile. In the days since Lisa's death, he certainly needed smiles. He rang the doorbell.

Marta opened the door wearing a big smile. "Hi ya, stranger!"

Greg took her in his arms and gave her a warm kiss, "Sorry, about that. We can make up for it in the coming weeks."

The lady with the puppies lived close by, on the edge of town. She had a kennel at her home. The puppies were adorable, even cuter than Tinker Bell. Knowing they were coming, the lady had brought them into the house. There were two females and one male. The male was two shades of brown with the most adorable little face ever. He was wearing a tiny, red collar. The lady believed in getting them used to a collar early. The puppies were comical trying to run on the glossy, kitchen vinyl. The little male would run as fast as his short legs allowed and then go sliding on his tummy, when his feet slid out from under him. Greg picked him up in one hand, remarking how small he was. The puppy seemed to take to him immediately. Marta watched, noticing how content Greg was as he held the little puppy. "You want a turn holding this loveable little thing?" Greg handed him to Marta. The puppy got excited, licked her hand, scurried up her arm, and began licking her face. Greg laughed, thinking he wasn't the only one who was fond of Marta. There was no doubt that Maggie would fall in love with this puppy. This was definitely the puppy for her. Greg made arrangements to pick up the puppy Christmas Eve day and take it to Marta's. She would bring it to the house early Christmas morning.

Marta was a huge help with the shopping. Her taste was excellent, of course—again, so much like Lisa's. She had a wonderful idea for Maggie. She suggested a little doggie coat for the puppy. As much as she loved dressing her dolls, they knew she would love the doggie coat idea. They found a red one to match the puppy's little collar. The coat had a matching red hat with elastic under the chin. They laughed, knowing how the puppy would love this! The sales lady in the toy store offered suggestions for Maggie's age, as Marta and Greg were both a little out of touch in the toy department. Of course, they bought a new doll. The clerk had showed them one that was very popular this season. Marta found an adorable doll buggy, which Maggie was sure to love.

On the way home, they picked up a pizza, smothered with all the toppings, not having to worry a mushroom or olive might land on Maggie's piece, as she was spending the night at Lori and Steve's.

After pizza, they decided to relax in the Jacuzzi. This would be something new for Marta. Greg brought out the chilled wine and set it on the ledge of the Jacuzzi, along with two glasses. He opened a fresh bag of strawberries 'n cream potpourri and sprinkled it about on the ledge. By the time the tub filled, the room had the fragrance of a strawberry patch on a warm summer day. Greg opened the little refrigerator and brought out a bowl of fresh strawberries and a can of whipped cream—placing them on the ledge. He drew Marta near. "You feel soo good." He kissed her—a long, slow kiss—feeling her voluptuous breasts pillowing against his chest. He tried not to rush things, although the thought of seeing her magnificent body again got his blood pumping. He watched, practically panting, as she slowly removed her clothes. He stepped out of his jeans, revealing a midnight blue thong, which left little to the imagination. Marta almost gasped at the sight of him. She took the elastic in her teeth, slowly sliding them down his thighs to completely expose him. Oh, how she wanted him. He removed his shirt, took her hand and helped her in. He sat down beside her and poured a glass of chilled chardonnay for each of them. They sipped the wine, while nibbling on strawberries and whipped cream.

So this is what couples do with strawberries and whipped cream. She had always been curious, thinking there was something more to it.

She laid her head back and slid her body down. There she lay, just under the surface of the clear bubbly water. The jets were on low, allowing Greg to see her overwhelmingly beautiful body. As he was absorbing all this beauty, he was unaware that she was also admiring the effect her beauty was having on him. They lay back quietly talking, each knowing they were falling in love. As they were involved in a passionate kiss, their heads slipped under the water. They came up choking and laughing. The mood had been broken for the time being, and they decided to get out of the Jacuzzi.

Greg watched her dry off, noticing the curves being in all the right places. She was lovely, inside and out. He slipped on a pair of leopard print bikini briefs and grabbed a robe to lounge in. He was intrigued, to say the least, with Marta's choice—a semi-sheer Magenta nightie, which stopped just above her thighs. His eyes were fixed on her, as she slid on matching bikini panties. He suddenly was becoming interested in continuing where they left off. How could he have thought the fun was over?

They took the spiral staircase down to the grand drawing room, passing by the beautiful Christmas tree, which remained free of any crimson substance, although the memory would forever be stamped in their minds. They sat side by side on the sofa in the parlor catching up on the last two weeks. Greg told her how Maggie was being even less sociable. He felt as if something was drawing her to the sewing room more and more all the time. He was hopeful the new puppy would take care of this problem.

Greg's attention was focused on the sexy bikini panties he knew Marta was wearing. When he could no longer dismiss his desires, he knelt on the floor in front of her. He began to massage her feet, kissing her ankles, slowly working his way up to her thighs, where he stopped. He kissed her love mound through her magenta panties, and began kissing his way down the other thigh. When he reached her ankle, he softly whispered, teasing, "What is it you want, sweetie?"

She was beyond answering. He knew she was at the point where rational thought ceased and physical sensations ruled. He slowly eased her panties off with his teeth, dangling them in front of her…again teasing…wanting to take her up another notch. Reaching under her, he pulled her forward, and dropped the panties from his teeth. Her eyes told him she was on fire with desire. When he touched her little nub with his thumb she soared into flight. He lifted her off the sofa and laid her on the floor in front of the glowing fireplace, where he threw his robe aside, stripped off his bikini briefs, and took them both far beyond the realm of imagination.

Eight

"Daddy, wake up! It's time to get up and see what Santa brought!"

Greg rolled over and looked at the digital alarm clock on the bedside stand. "Maggie, it's only four o'clock!"

"I know. It's time to get up!" she begged, as she tugged on the covers.

Greg knew he couldn't win this one. He eased his way to the edge of the bed and planted his feet on the floor.

"Here, Daddy, here's your slippers." As he put his feet into the slippers, she threw his robe at him. Greg's eyes were hardly open enough to see how cute Maggie looked. She was bubbly and all smiles, practically pulling him down the spiral staircase. She let go of his hand when she spied the little doll buggy. She oohed and aahed over it and ran back up the stairs to get one of her dollies, returning with three. "I couldn't decide which one to bring, so I brought all these. I wanted them all to have a ride in my new buggy."

Greg sat in his favorite chair and watched while she strolled down the hall and back, doing figure eights through the grand drawing room and back down the hall again. This time she disappeared into the sewing room. He could hear her talking excitedly. He wondered if she was talking to her dollies or the imaginary friend he had concluded she had in the sewing room. As she came back into the parlor, he noticed a ray of light beside her. At second glance, he also saw a smaller ray of light beside the larger one.

We have got to get out of this house before it drives me totally nuts, Greg thought to himself. There seemed to be no answers, other than the house was haunted. He had resigned himself to the fact that whatever it was, it was there to cause no harm to them, only discomfort with the fact that something was far from normal in this house.

As Greg waited for Marta to arrive, he turned on some Christmas music while he watched Maggie play. She had begged to open more presents, and he had convinced her to wait until Marta arrived. Maggie settled in the sewing room with her dolls. Greg dozed until he heard Marta pull into the drive at seven. Maggie was so involved with her dolls that she didn't hear her drive up. Greg ran to the back servants' entrance to greet her. He took the puppy carrier from her hand. The pup had fallen asleep in the jeep and was now beginning to wake up. Hoping the pup would stay quiet for a while, Greg draped a small cover over the carrier and hid it in the hall by the cellar way.

Maggie heard them coming in through the kitchen and excitedly ran to greet Marta, knowing she could now open more gifts. Marta was dressed exquisitely in an off-white, wool, straight skirt and red, cashmere sweater, making Greg feel under dressed. He was still clad in his robe. Marta, of course, didn't mind, because he looked sexy in anything, and she could only imagine what he was, or wasn't, wearing under the robe.

Maggie was as cute as a kitten, in a pink fleece robe Lisa had purchased at an after Christmas sale, just the year before. It fit perfectly now. Marta bent down to give her a hug, which lasted about two seconds before she took Marta's hand and began dragging her to the grand drawing room to the unopened gifts. So far, there were no little barks or whines from the servants' entrance. Now, at the other end of the house, they would be sure not to hear the puppy if he began making noises.

They continued to be amazed at how beautiful the tree was, remembering how it had been dripping with the red substance a few days earlier. It remained a mystery as to how it had disappeared so completely, without Maggie ever knowing there was a problem.

Before Greg and Marta could get seated, Maggie was tearing the wrapping paper off of another gift. "Ohhh, how cute!" She tucked the new doll into the buggy with the older dolls and strolled back down the hallway. She came running back as fast as she could guide the buggy, "Daddy, Daddy, I hear something in the back hall. It...it sounds like a barking noise!"

Marta and Greg looked at each other, almost laughing. "Let's go check this out. Maybe it's just the wind." Greg suggested.

"No, Daddy, I know it's not the wind. It sounded like Tinker Bell."

"Maybe Lori and Steve are here. It might be Tinker Bell."

As they approached the back hall, the barking sounds became louder. Maggie got more excited. She knew it wasn't Lori and Steve. She spied the draped carrier as soon as Greg opened the door to the hall. She looked up at Greg, with the biggest grin, ran over to the carrier, and quickly pulled the cover off.

There she saw the little brown and tan pup looking up at her, wiggling, barking, as if to say "Get me out of here, pick me up!" Greg opened the door of the carrier, and the puppy ran directly to Maggie. Greg had never seen Maggie so happy. She picked the puppy up and held him closely as he wiggled and licked her adorable, smiling face.

"Where's his basket?" Maggie asked.

"What basket are you talking about?" Greg asked.

"One like in the Wizard of Oz!"

"Why do you ask that?"

"You don't know, Daddy?"

"Afraid I don't, honey. I guess you'll have to explain it to me."

"Look at him, Daddy. He looks just like Toto in Wizard of Oz! And, Toto rides in a basket on the bicycle!"

"Oh, I guess he does!" He now understood the need for a basket. "So, what is this puppy's name?" he teased.

"Daddy, you know, don't you? It's Toto, of course!"

It never ceased to amaze Greg how quickly Maggie always came up with such cute, appropriate names.

Needless to say, Toto was the center of attention for a while. Greg and Marta sat and watched, as they talked quietly, Marta still curious as to what was under Greg's robe.

Toto became interested in the ribbons on the gifts under the tree. This gave Maggie a renewed interest in opening the rest of her gifts. "Time to stop the kissy, kissy stuff and open presents."

Toto helped Maggie remove the red ribbon from the package containing the red knit doggie coat. He wiggled and squirmed as Maggie put the little coat on him. It was a little big for him—hilariously cute, nevertheless. Maggie loved it. They laughed watching him try to take the hat off, which didn't take long, as it was too large for him. Maggie rode him around in her buggy, until he jumped out and slid across the hardwood floor, bringing giggles from all. He was even cuter than Tinker Bell.

Suddenly, Marta jumped up from the sofa and walked toward the hall, "I almost forgot. I left some gifts in the back hall." She returned with two attractively wrapped gifts. She handed the larger one to Maggie; of course she was delighted with another gift to open. Toto grabbed hold of the blue, glittery ribbon, which was curled tightly as if it had been hand curled with a scissor blade. The beautiful ribbon quickly became only fragments of a bow.

Maggie was thrilled to see the gift was a bed for Toto. "Thanks, Marta. We need one of these!"

Greg smiled, "Yes, Mart, it's a good thing somebody is thinking!" He brought a gift out from under the tree and handed this last one to Marta. "Merry Christmas, sweetie."

Marta, wearing a glowing smile, handed him a gift.

"Ladies first," said Greg, also smiling.

Greg's gift to her was beautifully wrapped from an expensive department store, which she immediately recognized. She lifted the tissue paper to find a beautiful, sleek, black dress—her correct size.

"Perhaps you can wear it New Year's Eve when we go to The Towers."

"Really, we are going there?" Marta knew

reservations had to be made well in advance, because it was an extremely popular, elite nightclub.

"Yep, I made the reservations weeks ago."

"And you assumed I would go with you?" she teased.

Greg was grinning that sexy smile of his. "Was that presumptuous of me?"

"Well...not really." She gave him a quick kiss, one that she would have loved to pursue, but Maggie was there, and Greg had a gift to open yet.

Greg slowly removed the ribbon, then the paper. "Now, what can this be?" He recognized the name of the jewelry store on the small box. He lifted an exquisite watch from the box. "Marta, you shouldn't have. This is great, such a handsome watch. This will definitely be for special occasions, such as New Year's Eve."

Knowing the gifts had all been opened, Maggie suddenly lost interest, "I'm hungry, Daddy, we forgot to have breakfast."

"Forgot? Not really, it isn't much past breakfast time now. Remember, we have been up since four!"

"Oh, my, that early?" Marta laughed, remembering how she used to get her mom up at extremely early hours on Christmas morning. She would try to convince her, with no avail, to go back to bed for a while. Once, she pretended to go back to bed and snuck into the living room and played with her new dollhouse for some time, before returning to beg her again to get up. She acted surprised to see the dollhouse, but her mom knew. She hadn't hid a thing from her. The furniture in the dollhouse had been rearranged. Her mom told her years later she had known. Then there was the year that she ruined

Christmas for herself. She found a large box hidden in her mom's closet. One by one, she examined each gift until she knew every Christmas gift she would receive. That was the last year she snooped. She had learned her lesson.

Greg interrupted her thoughts with, "Who wants pancakes?"

"Meee", squealed Maggie, as she skipped into the kitchen with Toto in one arm, her new doll in the other.

She was far ahead of Greg and Marta, as they stayed behind to enjoy a long passionate kiss.

"Later," smiled Greg. "Maybe we can convince Maggie to spend the night with Lori and Steve, so Toto and Tinker Bell can spend a little time together."

"Great idea! Then if I'm not being too presumptuous, I can spend the night...in your bed?"

"That you can, sweetie! For now we need to scurry into the kitchen and whip up some pancakes."

They had expected to find Maggie in the kitchen setting the table. Instead she was in the sewing room, seemingly introducing Toto and Dorothy, the new doll, to her invisible friend. Even on Christmas, there was no break from the invisible friend.

Marta quickly mixed up the pancake batter. Greg got out the syrup and set the table. Maggie soon came bouncing in. "We need two more chairs for my new friends."

"You mean one more. Puppies don't sit at the table. Why don't you go get his pretty blue doggie bed and put it over there in the corner? He must be tired from all the excitement. He has played hard. He needs some rest before we go to Aunt Lori and Uncle Steve's for dinner."

"Oh, goodie! Toto can meet Tink!" She laid

Dorothy on a chair and put Toto down on the floor and ran down the hall, with an exhausted Toto trailing her. Maggie met him half way down the hall on her way back with his doggie bed. She picked him up and carried him back to the kitchen and placed him on the bed. Surprisingly, he stayed while she sat Dorothy on a pillow on a chair beside her. Marta set a plate of two small pancakes, topped with strawberries, in front of Maggie.

Toto settled down and fell asleep. By the time Maggie finished her pancakes and milk, her eyelids were drooping. It wasn't even her normal time to get up yet, and she had already been up for four hours. Greg himself was feeling a little droopy. He convinced Maggie to go lie on the sofa by the Christmas tree. He and Marta would clean up the kitchen. They quickly finished and retired to the parlor. "Finally, we are alone. Well, sort of." Greg put his arm around Marta and snuggled up close. It was always difficult waiting until he could be alone with her. Desires had been mounting since she had arrived. Greg got up, closed, and locked the door. Surely Maggie was asleep by now, in the next room. He sat down beside Marta and opened his robe, which revealed a sheer, red, string thong and one terrific piece of equipment.

"Oh, Greg," Marta moaned.

He tossed the thong, wasting no time, as they were both very ready, and they couldn't be sure how long Maggie would stay asleep. He laid her down and partially undressed her; placing his knees between her thighs he spread them. This alone, took her up a notch. As he took himself deep within her, her hips began moving sensually to his rhythm. She was being taken higher and higher, until she soared, flying through a bright, color drenched universe, where Greg joined her, exhausted.

They lay quietly, catching their breath, until Greg broke the silence. "God, that was good! Wow, what we do to each other!" He gave Marta a sweet, loving kiss. "I need to go take a shower," he said, as he put his robe on. "Do you want to shower?"

"I should. Would you check on Maggie? I certainly don't want her to catch us."

Greg went around the corner to the grand drawing room to find Maggie fast asleep. He returned to Marta. "The coast is clear, let's go up the back stairs so we won't wake her. I'll use the master bath. The shower seems to be working okay now. Just in case, you better take the other one. Here, wrap this throw around you." As they passed the kitchen, they noticed Toto was still asleep in his bed.

They quickly showered, dressed, and got back downstairs before Maggie awoke. Toto was stirring. They decided to let Maggie sleep a little longer so they could have some quiet time to talk. They returned to the parlor and made sure they hadn't left any signs of lovemaking. Marta fluffed the decorator pillows on the sofa. All was in order now. They were almost afraid to sit close again, after what just happened. "Do we dare?" Marta asked Greg.

"Who knows, the way things work with us?" They both chuckled. Greg moved close to Marta, put his arm around her, and drew her closer. Their lips met. Greg so loved her soft lips and everything else about her. He loved how she made him feel. He did ask himself though, "Is it just sex with Marta, or can I possibly be falling in a sort of love with her?" He wasn't comfortable with either answer. He knew Lisa was his love.

Maggie came into the room rubbing her eyes. "Where's Toto?"

At that moment Greg caught sight of a red string hanging from the back of a chair. He felt a sense of panic, thinking Maggie might see it, and go over to it, to get a better look. How would he explain this? She knew nothing of men's sexy underwear and that was nothing he was ready to educate her on. He could only hope she wouldn't see it. He tried not to direct her attention to the chair or the red string. He looked straight at Maggie as he answered, "He's still asleep in the kitchen. He must have been worn out."

Maggie left the room, and turned toward the kitchen. Greg wasted no time grabbing his string thong and stuffing it in his pants pocket. Meanwhile, Maggie found Toto off his bed and stretching. She picked him up and went into the sewing room, where he leapt from her arms and began running around circling the wooden rocker and barking at it. As Greg and Marta approached the room, they heard Maggie saying, "It's okay, they are nice people. You don't need to bark at them."

Oh, my, there is more than one of them. He let Maggie know he was there when he said, "Maggie, it's time for you to get dressed to go to Aunt Lori and Uncle Steve's."

"I'll come upstairs and help you pack a bag in case you and Toto decide to spend the night," Marta chimed.

"Don't forget Dorothy. She will want to stay, too!" Maggie reminded Marta.

Greg smiled, thinking Marta had paved the way to some alone time...the entire night! Marta was also smiling that same smile.

Maggie was anxious to show Toto and Dorothy to Lori and Steve. She was at their door before Greg and Marta had barely gotten out of the car. Greg went around to the back of the Tahoe and gathered up the gifts they had for Lori and Steve. Steve was holding the door for them. "Come on in, the pups are getting acquainted. Your little Toto sure is a cutie."

The house smelled wonderful. The aroma of ham and cherry pie took over the house. Marta set the homemade rolls, which she had made the day before, on the counter. "We will probably want to warm these."

Lori agreed, "As soon as I take the ham out of the oven, we can put them in. I'm sure they'll be yummy."

And they were. Everything was delicious. They all seemed to be enjoying their time together. Although Greg was sure everyone was thinking of Lisa and how much life she always brought to the party. He tried not to think too hard. Lisa deserved the thoughts, but he knew she wouldn't want him to dwell on her and what couldn't be. Marta was becoming very important to him. She helped him enjoy life more than he ever thought would be possible after losing Lisa. He and Lisa had a perfect love—the kind so few ever find. And now, he felt he was beginning to experience another love like few ever find. Marta truly was a lot like Lisa. Lisa had known this, just as she knew it could be possible for Greg to love Marta, as he had loved her.

They weren't sure who enjoyed the gift exchange more. They laughed thinking the pups enjoyed playing with the gift-wrap, as much as the rest of them enjoyed seeing the gifts they received.

The two pups romped and played all afternoon.

They were so cute together. Toto jumped up on Greg's lap, wanting Greg to play with him and the wadded up wrapping paper. He really was an active little pup, teasing Greg with the paper. As he jumped down onto the floor and began scurrying across the room toward the kitchen, Greg noticed something red hanging from Toto's mouth. He almost gasped. No one else seemed to notice as Tinker Bell had caught their eye as she played with a rubber toy, looking exceptionally cute. Greg immediately got up and followed Toto into the kitchen where Steve was getting a drink of water. Toto dropped the red thong at Steve's feet.

"Hey boy, what do we have here?" Steve examined the red fabric and almost burst out laughing as he looked over at Greg entering the room. "This wouldn't happen to be yours, would it?"

Greg had totally forgotten about the thong, after he became so disturbed over discovering Maggie was talking to more than one invisible person. "I suppose it could be," Greg said blushing.

"Any idea how Toto got it," Steve said, laughing.

Greg quietly explained how he had quickly stuffed it in his pocket after the earlier incident. He knew Steve would never let him forget this. They were both glad no one else had noticed.

Lori and Steve were happy to have Maggie and Toto spend the night. Greg brought Toto's bed and carrier in from the Tahoe, although Lori felt it probably wasn't necessary, as they could share Tinker Bell's bed. Tinker Bell was so well behaved that they didn't use the carrier anymore, except for travel. Of course, they didn't know how Toto would behave. Greg, especially, hoped Toto would behave. He made sure his red thong wasn't left behind for a repeat of the incident.

*

As Greg and Marta drove off, Marta was trying to imagine how it would be to have Greg all to herself for the night. It didn't happen often enough for her. He, too, had been dreaming about this night for some time. In his thoughts he planned a very romantic evening with wine, candlelight, the Jacuzzi, and, of course, Marta. When they arrived, he led Marta upstairs. The Jacuzzi filled as he poured the wine. With their glasses in hand, they sat on the bed quietly sipping their wine, while slowly undressing each other. He soon was wearing only a see through white string thong and she a red nylon thong—each a tremendous turn on for the other. Marta's desires intensified as she eyed his growing progression, especially in that sexy thong. He sipped the last of his wine and gently laid her back, pulling her thong to the side to expose her clean-shaven lips, something new in recent weeks. He knew how to tease, and was deliberate in his approach, bringing her to the point of no return. Tonight he would take his time. The night was theirs, and they would make the most of it. His passionate tongue and magical fingers began taking her there too fast. He took her hand and pulled her to her feet, watching the thong strap settle into place—wanting, needing.

He led her into the bathroom. She let out a shrill scream at the sight of the Jacuzzi—now a bubbling blood bath, almost ready to run over the sides. It appeared to be clear coming from the faucet, turning into a substance resembling blood as it touched the bubbling mixture. Greg quickly turned the faucet off, and the substance stopped just as it reached the top of the Jacuzzi, continuing to bubble to a rapid boil. He led Marta back to the bedroom and slammed the door. He couldn't be sure the bloody substance wouldn't overflow, although he couldn't stand there and watch.

Should they leave the house, go to the parlor for the night, or sleep in the spare bedroom? Marta agreed to try the spare bedroom, as the picture was now back in the mansard, and for some time there had been no activity in the mansard stairway, around the corner from this room. After all, whatever was causing all these mysterious happenings had not harmed anyone. They pulled the covers back and crawled in, leaving their underwear on—just in case! The mood had definitely been broken by the Jacuzzi's mysterious substance. Greg held Marta closely, as she snuggled next to him—no passion—only closeness. Sleep finally came after several hours of soft whispering, not to be overheard by anyone or anything.

Greg awoke early and decided to check on the Jacuzzi while Marta slept. He let out a yell when his foot hit the floor. It felt like he was stepping in a puddle of water. He was almost afraid to look down.

Marta awoke with Greg's yell, "What's wrong, honey?"

When he looked down, he found he was standing in a clear liquid resembling water. "Sweetie, the floor is wet. I'm not sure why."

"Is it red?" she asked, looking over the edge of the bed. Her eyes followed the clear liquid up the wall—she screamed, "The portrait is back!"

Greg glanced over at the wall. The portrait indeed was back on the nail where they had hung it weeks before. The girl in the portrait was crying. Tears were running down the picture onto the wall and onto the floor. Greg was standing in a huge puddle of tears. "Here we go again! I thought we had her put away where she wouldn't bother us anymore. Maybe we should burn the picture this time."

"No, we need to keep it—at least until we can determine who she is and hopefully why and how she cries tears," Marta disagreed.

"Okay, how about if I take it to the carriage house? Not that I care to go in there. I haven't been in there for a while. Hard telling what I might find in there." He went down the back stairs, with Marta on his heels, and grabbed some rags from the cellar way, returning to wipe up the wet substance. He was tempted to taste it to see if it was salty like tears.

Just as he was ready to touch his finger to his tongue, Marta screamed. "No…what do you think you are doing? We have no idea what that substance is. It might be poisonous!"

"I guess, you're right. I'll pass on the taste test. I don't think I'm ready to die yet. Before this happened, I was headed down the hall to check on the Jacuzzi. Care to come along?"

"No, but I certainly don't want to stay here, either. I'll come with you. I need to get some clean clothes out of my bag anyway. I left it in your room when we tore out of there last night."

They quietly walked down the hall, not to disturb whatever was causing the Jacuzzi mystery. Greg slowly opened the bathroom door. Everything looked perfectly normal—as if the red substance never existed.

"Now, why am I surprised? I should know by now that any red substance that appears mysteriously has a way of disappearing just as mysteriously." They quickly dressed. "Do you want breakfast before I go to the carriage house?"

"No, I doubt that I could eat now anyway. And, it isn't you—it is we going to the carriage house. I am not staying in this house alone. I may not go into the carriage house, though. I will go as far as the door with you."

Greg gave Marta a peck on the lips and led her back to the spare bedroom. He took the picture from the nail on the wall and stared at it a few seconds, then turned to Marta, "Ready for our next adventure?"

Marta grabbed his hand, and they went down the back stairway. As they passed the door to the mansard, Marta thought she heard the sound of a baby crying. She wondered if it was her imagination. Greg said nothing about hearing it, so she kept quiet. As they neared the carriage house, they both became extremely nervous. Neither spoke as Greg slowly opened the door wide enough for them to peek in. It looked fine. He stepped inside. Marta followed.

Greg looked back at her, "Think we should put it in the tack room?"

"I'd rather just leave it here. Knowing you though, you will go back into the tack room. Then if all is okay in there, you will venture back to the stable to check it out."

Marta was right. Greg slowly proceeded to the tack room, holding the picture in one hand, with Marta tightly squeezing his other hand. All looked okay in the tack room, so he insisted they go to the stable. It, too, seemed okay. Greg didn't open the trap door above. "No sense pushing our luck, let's head back."

"Remember to leave the portrait," Marta reminded.

Greg took one last look at the picture. He kissed the girl in the portrait on the lips. "Good-bye missy, have a nice rest out here." He turned and headed toward the door, locking the padlock on the door as he left.

"Why did you kiss the picture?" Marta inquired.

"Just teasing. I guess it wasn't a very good thing to do," Greg answered.

Marta was uneasy and in a hurry to get back to the house. Why she felt the house was any safer, she wasn't sure. "I wish we could find some clue as to who this girl in the picture is. Maybe we need to go back into the mansard to see if we can come up with something."

"Not today, sweetie. We have had enough excitement already for one day."

"Greg, honey, did you happen to hear a baby crying as we passed by the door to the mansard?"

"I was hoping I was imagining it, guess not, huh?" Greg replied.

"I guess not, as I know I heard it. I hated to mention it at the time, as there was enough going on. When you have heard it before, do you think it has come from the mansard?" Marta asked.

"It has never been very loud, and by the time I get near the source, it has stopped."

They decided to spend the night at Marta's. Lori and Steve agreed to keep Maggie and Toto for another night. They packed a few things and sat in the parlor talking until they began to get hungry. They decided on lunch, as it was now too late for breakfast.

After lunch they went to the library and looked for books on haunted houses and spirits. Each of them checked out several to study. Afterward, they went to Marta's and tried to relax and not think about the mysteries of the house. This proved to be impossible. They spent the afternoon scanning the books looking for clues. After several hours, they set the books aside, deciding they needed to take a break. Tomorrow they would venture into the mansard once again.

Nine

"Are you sure you want to do this?" Greg asked Marta, as they stood in front of the mansard door.

"We need to find out who this girl is and why her portrait cries tears. It's the only place I know where we might find some clues," Marta answered.

As Greg opened the door, they began to hear the cries of a baby. More than likely this is where the cries had been coming from all along. Greg led the way with Marta following closely. There was no sign of a baby, not that they really expected to see a real baby. The cries stopped.

"Well, I guess that's that for now," Greg said. "We need to add a baby to our list of clues to search for. Where should we look today?"

"How about the bedroom across the hall from where we searched last time, where we found the box of pictures?" Marta suggested.

Greg looked as if he was thinking hard, "We didn't finish in there did we?"

"You are right. Once we found the box, we decided to take it downstairs to look through it. Maybe there are more boxes in there that might lead us to our answers."

With all the dust and cobwebs, it was difficult to tell at a glance what really was in there. Greg opened a closet, close to where they found the last box. There were three boxes filled with papers, pictures, and possibly old letters. "Look Marta, these boxes might help us find some answers. How about if I put them by the stairs while we look around some more up here? We can take them down when we go."

"Sounds good to me. It's freezing cold up here. We shouldn't waste our time on just a few boxes. We need to see what else we can find before we get too cold to stay up here." Marta wandered to the other side of the room, where she found some old dishes. "Honey, these must be worth a fortune, they look really old."

"Like most of the things up here," Greg chuckled.

"One thing that surprises me is that these things appear to belong to the family that lived downstairs years back. Why are these things still here? I would have thought the previous owners would have gotten rid of all these things, or that they would have been cleared out before the house was sold. If this used to be the living quarters for the female servants, do you suppose there are some remains of their belongings up here, too?" Marta questioned.

"That's quite possible, Marta. Are you ready to move on to the other bedrooms?"

"Sure, we can come back to this room later. I'm curious as to how the other rooms look." Marta headed for the bedroom across the hall. Greg followed.

In this room, they found a twin bed covered with a handmade quilt, all white with delicate stitches embroidered in a repetitious pattern. The fabric was rotten, and tore when Marta attempted to pick it up.

In a far corner of this room, there was an oval

shaped metal container, which looked like an old watering trough. It contained what appeared to be the remains of an old feather pillow with a pillowcase covering it, rotten and in shreds. A small bed cover, similar to the quilt on the twin bed, was folded at one end. "Greg, honey, do you suppose this was used as a bed for a small child?"

"Or a baby?" Greg quickly added.

"Oh my gosh! You may be right! This could be a crib for the baby we have heard crying."

"Let's not draw any conclusions yet, Mart. Let's see what the next room brings." He headed down the hall with Marta trailing. This room had three twin beds, all stripped down to old feather mattresses. There was more dust and cobwebs than anything else in this room, with no apparent clues. They moved on to the next room.

This room was quite full. It looked to be the main storage room. The closet was full of old time dresses, covered with yellowed and rotted sheets. Marta carefully took the sheets off to get a better look at them. She assumed they must have been quite elegant in their time. Some of them had a piece of yellowed, brittle paper pinned to them, seeming to label the owner of each dress. There were names such as Josephine, Isadora, Edith, Lizzie, and Rosalina.

Greg was rummaging through things stacked against one wall. "Look Marta. Here are more portraits, some are on porcelain and some are needlework." Marta rushed over to look at them. "Mart, look, this one is of a girl much younger than the one who cries. She bears a strong resemblance to the crying girl. What do you think?"

"If it isn't her, it's her twin. Those eyes are

definitely hers, so is the nose. Oh, yes, it must be her. I don't suppose we would be so lucky as to find a name on the back," Marta said, excitedly.

Greg carefully removed the elegant gold frame to expose the back. Isadora was clearly written on the back of the portrait. "We should compare this with the smudged name on the back of the other picture." He took off to get the picture and was back in a second, removing it from the frame.

Marta held the handwritten name, Isadora, up to it. "Look, Greg, the letters o-r-a are quite clear. Only the beginning letters are blurred."

"Hmmm…so her name is Isadora."

Marta wasn't totally convinced yet, "Let's look at the two pictures side by side."

They held them up together. Greg studied them carefully, "Look at those cheekbones; they are so much alike. The eyes and hair are both the same color. The nose is identical. Even the smile is similar. Yes, it looks like we have our girl. Where did we put that bible?" Greg again took off down the hall, returning with the bible. He turned to the back where the names were written. Yes, the name Isadora was one of the names.

Marta's face lit up. "I think that was one of the names on some of the dresses I found in the closet." She went over to the closet and began looking through the dresses. "Yes, here it is! This one is labeled Isadora! Honey, bring that bible over here. Let's see if the rest of the names on these dresses match." Sure enough, they matched the girls' names written in the bible. There were a few more girls' names than dresses. The names on the dresses were all there in the bible.

"I think we have found all we need for today, Marta. Ready to go downstairs?"

"Sure, I'm getting too cold, anyway. We must not forget to take those boxes we saved for later."

Greg grabbed the boxes and they headed toward the stairs, making sure he left the two portraits behind. "Two of these could flood the whole house," he teased, as he laid them against some boxes.

*

Once downstairs, they decided to shower. They were covered with dust and cobwebs. While in the shower, it hit Greg that Maggie's birthday was in two days, and they hadn't made any plans. As he was drying off, Marta came in from the main bath wrapped in a towel. She had no desire to shower in the master bath. Greg still chanced it. He wanted to keep check on it. What a temptation that was for Greg, as the towel dropped to the floor, and she began dressing.

Instead of saying something sexy, he informed Marta, "Mart, I almost forgot Maggie's birthday is day after tomorrow. I need to get with it, do some shopping, and make some plans."

"Can I help?" she asked, as she was repositioning her breasts in her lavender bra.

"Oh, can you!" he laughed. "Do you know how difficult you are making this for me? I need to get some shopping done, and yes, you can go with me. I was wondering if we could find a basket for Toto, like Maggie mentioned Christmas. Do you know what kind of basket that might be?"

"Yes, it's one that has a lid. I think I know what the one in the movie looks like."

"Do you suppose any store would have anything similar? You know Maggie; she would get a kick out of something like that. Remember, Christmas she asked where his basket was?"

"I know where there is a specialty basket shop downtown Galena. They might have something close to it."

"Great! We could eat at one of the little restaurants there on Main Street. Lis…" he stopped himself.

"Yes, I know, Lisa loved those little shops. We used to eat at one of the restaurants when we would take a fun day to see what was new at the little shops. Maybe we should eat somewhere else. What do you think?"

"Have you eaten at that new little place in the park area?" Greg asked. "It has only been there a month or so, I believe."

"That's right," Marta said, "there is a new little restaurant there. I only drove by it. I haven't eaten there. I hear what they mostly sell is specialty sandwiches."

"So, let's give it a try then," Greg was getting hungrier now.

They quickly dressed and were out the door. Greg was surprised he was actually able to resist that gorgeous body of hers. At times, he had wondered if he was a little oversexed. He was proud of himself that he had controlled his urges—this time. He knew, though, that it was only because there wasn't time. He had Maggie's birthday on his mind. He must get the shopping done before he picked her up from Lori and Steve's. The boxes from the mansard could wait.

The new sandwich shop was indeed a specialty shop. It fit right in with the area with all the other specialty shops. This was such a unique little town. Greg and Marta chose sandwiches with a yeast roll bun.

The bun really made the sandwich. They were baked fresh each morning, so the waitress said. There were many choices. Marta chose a peppered chicken and Greg had roast beef, Cajun style. They were quite pleased with this new shop, as both sandwiches were delicious.

Marta directed Greg to the basket shop. They had hundreds of baskets, each unique in its own way—all shapes, sizes, and colors. Marta described the Toto basket to the clerk. Sure enough, they had one very similar, the right size for Toto to grow into and not too terribly large for him now. The clerk found a box and gift-wrapped it in, yes, Wizard of Oz paper. Who would have thought!

"There's a little shop down the street where I need to go next," Greg hesitated a moment, "There is something I need to do for Lisa."

"You have me curious."

"You will see," Greg appeared quite serious.

Once inside the store, he studied the contents of a display case and pointed out a heart shaped photo locket to the clerk. He indicated to her the one he wanted. She put it in a small box and asked him if he would like it gift-wrapped? He thanked her and told her he would wrap it himself. He was so serious, so unlike how he had been lately. They drove home with hardly a word between them.

Once in the house, Greg finally began to explain, "I need to find a picture to put in this locket for Maggie—one of Lisa or maybe Lisa and Maggie together. There are some snapshots in the sewing room. Could you help me with this? I don't know that I can do it alone."

"Sure, Greg, I understand."

"No, you don't entirely. Lisa saw this last summer. She thought about getting it then, for Maggie's birthday. She knew if it were in the house, she would give it to her long before her birthday. We expected Lisa to still be here on Maggie's birthday." There were tears in his eyes. Marta had seen him cry only a few times since they had been together. Today was very different. He was allowing himself to think. They found some envelopes of snapshots. Ordinarily, Lisa would have had them in a photo album. Many things had been left undone.

"I want one of Lisa that looks like she did when she was well, not one to remind Maggie of how sick she was," Greg commented.

They looked at many pictures. Some were too large for the locket; others were too distant and therefore too small. They found two that would work. Greg was torn as to which one to use. He preferred one of the two of them together. The locket was hardly big enough for a picture of two, so he chose the one of Lisa alone. It was a wonderful picture of her and just the right size. He sat staring at it, hating to cut into the picture. Every few minutes he would wipe a tear away with his handkerchief. Eventually, he burst into tears. "I just can't believe she is gone, Mart!"

Marta had been trying hard to hold the tears back. She now joined him, and they comforted each other. It was good that they had each other, as they both loved Lisa, of course in different ways. Marta found Lisa's small sewing scissors and handed them to Greg, once he was able to continue. He first cut out a piece of paper about the size of the locket opening. He put it in the locket and found it was a little too big. He trimmed it until it fit perfectly and then used it for a pattern.

Once he had the picture in the locket, he sat staring at it, thinking how Maggie would surely treasure this, especially when she knew it was something Lisa had wanted to give her. He wrapped it, and then called to see if Maggie was ready to come home. He would pick her up soon.

"Marta, would you mind if I take you home on the way to pick up Maggie? I feel I should spend some time alone with her today."

"I understand Greg. We'll have plenty of time later to be together."

Greg kissed her good-bye at her door and gave her a big hug. He had tears in his eyes. Marta knew it had been a difficult day for him. She also sensed he was having mixed emotions about their new relationship.

*

Maggie was all smiles when he arrived at Lori and Steve's. "Daddy, Daddy, I missed you." She threw her arms around him and gave him a much-needed hug.

"Is Toto ready to go?" Greg asked Maggie.

"I think so. He needs a nap and Tinker bell won't let him take one!"

Greg thanked Lori and Steve for watching her, packed up Toto and Dorothy, and they were on their way.

Maggie ran to the house as fast as she could go. Greg followed carrying Toto, Dorothy, and Maggie's overnight bag. He set his baggage down and unlocked the door. Maggie went straight to the sewing room. As soon as Greg let Toto out of his carrier, he ran as fast as his little legs would carry him until he caught up with Maggie. Greg found Maggie standing, facing the rocking chair, and rambling on about her visit with Lori, Steve, and Tinker Bell. Greg could hardly make out what she was saying, because Toto was circling the rocking chair, barking.

"What in the heck is going on?" he asked himself. "Perhaps Toto is barking because Maggie is standing here talking to herself."

Toto soon settled down. Greg showed him his bed and gave him a little treat. He ate it and fell asleep. Greg asked Maggie if she could come into the parlor to talk about her birthday. She told her invisible friend she would be back later.

Maggie sat, Indian style, on one end of the sofa, "What do you think, Dad? What should we do for my birthday? I'm going to be 7 you know!"

"Yes, I know. You are getting so grown up. What would you like to do on your birthday?"

"Could we invite Amy and Kaitlyn to go to Gerry Giraffe's with us for pizza? You know I love those funny animals that sing. And the games, they are sooo fun!"

"Sure, honey, that sounds like fun to me. Would you like Marta to go, too?"

"Of course, Daddy. I like Marta. She is so much fun, like Mommy was. Can Toto come, too?"

"I'm afraid not, honey. Dogs aren't allowed in restaurants, not even cute little puppies like Toto."

"Not even if we keep him in his carrier?"

"No, honey. Not even if we keep him in the carrier. Imagine if everybody took his dog. They would all be barking at each other, running around jumping on the tables eating the pizza, and barking at the singing animals. It would be a wild mess and nobody would have any fun."

"Okay, Daddy. That does sound kinda wild. We want a fun party, don't we?"

She started to go toward the door. Greg asked, "Don't you want to stay here and talk more?"

"No, Daddy, I need to get back to the sewing room. I want to talk to Mommy some more, and Johnny needs me."

She skipped down the hall and turned into the sewing room. Greg was mystified. This wasn't getting any better. He decided to call Amy and Kaitlyn's parents to invite them to the party. Their moms accepted for them. Greg then decided to do some reading—this time in the sewing room. He sat in the overstuffed chair, reading one of the books he and Marta had checked out from the library, searching especially for anything about a red, sticky substance, flashes of light, crying babies, and crying portraits. At the same time he was watching and listening to Maggie.

Toto awoke and came wandering in. He again circled the wooden rocker barking at something, eventually settling down. Maggie picked him up and held him in her lap, as she read a book. She kept saying the name Johnny and talking in a more babyish talk. Once in a while she would look up and appear to be talking to someone else, these times using her normal voice. It certainly had Greg puzzled. One thing he did suspect was that a new puppy was not going to cure this problem. The library book wasn't giving him any answers either.

"Maggie, would you like some soup? It's about supper time."

"Sure, Daddy, have we got that good chicken noodle kind in a bag?"

"I believe we do. I'll go make some." He went into

the kitchen and started heating the water, still puzzled as to who Maggie was talking to. When it was done, he turned to call to Maggie, to tell her it was ready to eat. As he turned his head, for just a second he thought he saw a figure in the hall. The figure appeared to be that of a woman. There was a golden ray around her. He was a bit shaken, and at the same time, he felt an air of comfort. "Could that have been Lisa?" Greg asked himself. Oh, how he longed for her, especially at this moment.

Just then, Maggie came bouncing into the kitchen, "Daddy, something is boiling over. Is that my soup?" Greg quickly grabbed the handle of the pan and pulled it from the burner. While Maggie ate her soup, Greg made himself a sandwich, although his appetite had diminished.

After their little lunch, they retired to the sewing room. Greg had planned to spend the evening in the parlor. He had heard enough of the craziness in the sewing room. He was now drawn back to the sewing room. He wasn't sure what he saw in the hall. Maybe whatever or whoever it was would show up in the sewing room.

It was a long evening with no occurrences. Greg had hoped to see the glowing figure again. He needed to see if it was Lisa. There was no way he would forget what he saw—no way would he sleep tonight.

*

Maggie awoke early the next morning, knowing it was her birthday. She was excited to finally turn 7, and to be getting presents. Greg had decided to give her the locket first thing after breakfast. She was too excited to eat.

"Daddy, when do I get my presents?"

"I thought we would wait until your party. How would that be?" he teased.

"I am too excited to wait that long. Can I have them now?" she begged.

"I was hoping we could wait until Marta gets here for one of them. She helped me pick it out."

"Okay, Daddy, I will wait until later for one of them. Can I open one now, then?"

"Maggie, honey, I have one very special present from your mommy."

"Mommy didn't tell me she bought me a present!"

"I bought it for her, honey. I knew it was what she wanted you to have." Greg handed her the small package.

Maggie anxiously tore off the tiny pink bow and ripped the wrapping paper off. She opened the small, hinged box to find the locket. "Oh, Daddy! This is so adorable!"

This broke Greg's serious mood. Maggie was always surprising him with adult words. "Let me open it for you Maggie, honey."

Maggie smiled through her tiny tears, as she saw the picture of her mommy. "This is so special, Daddy. I love Mommy so much."

Greg told Maggie how Lisa had found it in one of the little shops and had planned to buy it for her for her birthday.

"Daddy, can you put it on me? I want to go show Mommy!"

Once Greg fastened the clasp around her neck, she flew off to the sewing room. He followed her. She stood in the middle of the room looking up, as if she was talking to someone.

"Mommy, Mommy...I love it. Thank you sooo much." She then blew a kiss into the air.

Greg was now convinced it was time to get help for her. He would ask her pediatrician for a recommendation.

Early afternoon, as Marta drove into the drive, she noticed something strange. The sky had been clear until she reached the house. Then, the house became engulfed in a dark cloud. She had never seen anything like it. There was no rain. There was a streak of light similar to lightning. It seemed to travel from the house to behind the house, near where the garden had been.

Maggie was excited to see Marta, and the present she had in her hand. It didn't take her long to talk Greg into letting her open the rest of the gifts. She was delighted with the Toto basket. "Oh, Daddy! It's just like in the Wizard of Oz!" She immediately put Toto in the basket. Much to her disappointment, he popped right back out.

"Maybe if you put a treat in it, he will like it better and stay in it awhile. It's new to him now. He will get used to it," Greg tried to sound convincing.

"I should have known he would jump out. Toto jumped out of the basket in the movie!"

"Yes, he did, but he wanted to find his way back to Dorothy, didn't he?" Greg asked.

"You're right, Daddy. So...maybe he will learn to like this basket," she smiled and tore into Marta's gift. "Oh, how precious!" she exclaimed. Marta had made an outfit for her new Dorothy doll. It was designed to look just like the pinafore Dorothy wore in the Wizard of Oz, right down to the shiny, red shoes. Maggie put the new clothes on Dorothy and tapped the dolls feet together just as Dorothy did in the movie when the Munchkins suggested this was her way home. Marta could tell how much Maggie liked her gift. She had made the clothes herself and found the shoes in a toy store.

Greg was smiling at Marta the entire time she was explaining how she had searched for just the right fabric to match the movie. Yes, in this way, too, she was like Lisa. Lisa would have done the same thing.

While Maggie played, Marta told Greg what she had seen, as she drove up. She took him outside to show him. The sky was clear. There were no clouds of any kind.

Maggie played with Dorothy and Toto until it was time for the party. She was getting a little frustrated with Toto, as even a treat didn't keep him in the new basket. Greg suggested she wait until he was a bit sleepy and try it later.

Greg and Marta sat nearby and talked while Maggie played. Of course, they snuck in a hug and kiss or two while she was absorbed in keeping Toto in the basket.

Greg hadn't forgotten what Marta had seen. He himself knew there was something mysterious about the flash of light he had seen that day so many months ago. He felt increasingly uneasy about staying in this house. The house had to be haunted. Was he pressing his luck by staying in the house? After the holidays, he would call a realtor to sell the house. He would find something smaller for him and Maggie, although he knew Maggie would be disturbed over leaving the house. The sewing room had become such an obsession with her. She wouldn't like leaving. Greg felt it would be best for her. Hopefully, her invisible friends would be lost in the move.

The pizza party was a fun time. The girls chattered and giggled all the way to Gerry Giraffe's. Greg was amazed at how much noise three little girls could make. They were tickled over the little zoo animals playing banjos, ukuleles, and singing on stage.

When they got home, Toto wasn't himself at all. He had chewed the matt in his carrier until there was nothing left except puffs of cotton and shreds of fabric. When Maggie opened the carrier, he shot out, totally ignoring her. Greg saw a streak of light disappear through the kitchen door. Toto seemed to be chasing after it. When it disappeared at the servants' entrance, Toto stood in front of the door and barked until he wore himself out and wobbled to his bed, where he fell asleep. Greg would call the realtor in the morning. He was now totally convinced they must leave.

Ten

Marta arrived soon after breakfast. She and Greg had decided to search through the contents of the box they had brought down from the mansard. Maggie was upstairs introducing Dorothy to her many dollies. Of course, Dorothy was the favorite for now. Toto was already asleep in the kitchen. He was worn out from his early morning stay in the basket training.

Greg met Marta at the door. "Hi, doll." He was all smiles. He put his arms around Marta and kissed her like they had been separated for months. She could sense his love for her was growing deeper. As they stood locked in each other's arms, Marta thought how wonderful it was that Lisa's plan was working. Greg was actually falling in love with her, something she never thought would happen after all these years of loving him; although she now realized she never really knew what love was before. How could she, as she had never been in his arms before and never felt his love in return? She thought about what makes true love so special—loving and being loved in return. Greg was the most thoughtful, loving, sensitive, and passionate guy she had ever known. To have him now made her the luckiest gal in the world.

Greg finally broke the embrace, "I guess if we are going to get to the bottom of these mysteries, we better get started on this box." He had it sitting on the kitchen table where they could go through it easier. Greg poured each of them a cup of coffee. "Want a bagel?"

"No, hon, I ate at home. Thanks for asking, though."

Greg sat down beside Marta, and they began to look through the box. He was thinking how he would rather be making love to her. He knew he must set those thoughts aside until later.

There were many old newspaper clippings, old letters, papers, and a booklet of some kind. Marta picked up the booklet and leafed through it. "Greg, sweetie, this looks like an old journal. It has the name Agatha Brown written in the front and many dated entries. They aren't daily entries, rather sporadic dates, but in chronological order."

"Why don't you read through that, while I look at some of these newspaper clippings? We might stumble across something here," Greg seemed to be settling into the search.

They were quiet for some time, each reading. Then, Greg looked up, "Remember our Isadora? This clipping tells of her death. She apparently died of tuberculosis at the young age of 20. Her last name was Stephens. Isn't that the name written in the bible we found?"

"Yes, I think so, sweetie," Marta answered.

"So, this backs up what we found earlier, only we had no idea she lived such a short life."

"Maybe that is why she cries in the portrait. Can spirits make a portrait cry?" Marta questioned.

"Well, something sure made our Isadora portrait

cry. What else could have done it, other than a spirit? I think our Isadora must be here in the house with us." Greg felt like they were finally getting somewhere.

"That's a scary thought. At least if she is here, she must be a good spirit. She was such a young lady, and she hasn't done anything to hurt us." Marta wanted to believe she was harmless.

Greg thought for a minute. "You don't suppose she was the one who raped me, do you?"

"Greg, how could she have raped you? She is a spirit. They only have spirit bodies, not actual flesh." Marta was trying to convince herself it was not possible.

"That's what I always thought. All I know is something, or somebody raped me that night. I didn't dream it. I woke up feeling the skin on my penis moving. I actually saw it moving!" he certainly hadn't forgotten that night.

"That is so weird, Greg. I guess I will have to take your word for it, since I wasn't there."

Marta began to read silently. She soon found something, "It looks like Agatha was a servant for the Stephens. She was one of the cooks."

"Keep reading, she might tell us something about the house." Greg leafed through more newspaper clippings, setting the one of Isadora's death aside.

Marta continued reading, until she found something else to share with Greg. "Agatha courted the chauffer, who lived above the stable. He was the last male servant. There had been two others, who had been let go, as they were no longer needed."

"Very interesting, keep reading." Greg prompted. Soon, he looked as if he found something else interesting, "Marta, sweetie, didn't Maggie tell us Johnny was in the sewing room with her?"

"Yes, that is what she said," Marta answered.

Greg looked up from the article he was reading. "Then, this is very interesting. This article tells of an 8 month old baby, by the name of Johnny Brown, who died when he fell down the mansard stairs."

Marta was astonished, "Oh my gosh! You don't suppose Maggie has been talking to this baby's spirit all this time?"

"Yeah, really mind boggling, isn't it!"

"Did you say his last name was Brown? That is Agatha's last name!" Marta exclaimed.

"Read fast, I think we may have something here. Remember, there is that bed upstairs, the right size for a baby. Wow!" Greg could hardly believe what they were finding.

They were again quiet, only the rustling of paper could be heard, until Marta let out a scream. "Here it is Greg! Agatha became pregnant by John the chauffer."

"And..." Greg coaxed Marta, anxious to hear more.

"I'm reading, I'm reading! John...Johnny that makes sense. Oh yes, here she says if it is a girl she will name her Mary, and if it is a boy, she will call him Johnny." Marta was excited to have found this.

"Well, what is he doing here with my Maggie?" Greg stopped reading, waiting for Marta to find some more answers.

"Yes, here it is. Agatha gave birth to a boy, upstairs in the mansard. One of the other female servants was with her. She stuck a rag in Agatha's mouth, so she couldn't be heard by anyone downstairs while she was laboring. How terrible," this disturbed Marta.

Greg couldn't believe what he was hearing, "That poor girl. Giving birth is difficult enough, without having a rag stuffed in your mouth!"

"Yes, imagine that! She tells of how the other servants watched Johnny for her while she worked her shift. Oh my gosh!" Marta could hardly believe what she had read.

"What?" Greg asked.

"Thirty minutes after Johnny was born, Agatha went downstairs and cooked supper for the Stephens' family!"

"How awful for her!" Greg continued to leaf through newspaper clippings while Marta read on.

"There were three other female servants, one other cook and two who cleaned for them. Their names were Althea, Bernice, and Lucinda." She continued to read aloud. "Here it is. She tells of Johnny's death after falling down the mansard steps. She is grieving terribly. So, now we know that it was the same Johnny."

Greg appeared to be very interested in one of the clippings, "Listen to this, Mart. Agatha Brown was murdered, stabbed to death by John Winchell!"

"How horrible!" Marta was astounded, by what they were finding.

"Yes, isn't it though?" Greg continued, "It says here that it happened in the servants' hallway late one night. She had been working late that night baking pies. He walked into the kitchen and grabbed a knife while they argued. She tried to escape from him, when he grabbed her in the back hall and stabbed her repeatedly in his furor. Bernice had been in the pantry and heard them arguing. He was furious that she hadn't watched Johnny better. He accused her of being a bad mother for letting him crawl so close to the stairs, which led to his death. Bernice was frightened for her life when he grabbed the knife. After they left the kitchen, she went to get help from the Stephens. When help came, it was too late. Agatha lay in the hallway in a pool of blood."

"Wow! This house has quite the history! What a horrible thing to happen!" Marta paused to think for a moment, "Greg, honey, isn't that where you found the red stuff one time?"

"You're right! You don't suppose there is a connection here?" Greg wondered.

"What else could it be? Somehow it must be connected. How blood can reappear after all these years, is beyond me!" Marta paused to think again, "Johnny died on the mansard stairs—also where we found the red substance. Yes, there must be a connection with these deaths!"

"Finally, we are putting some of the pieces of the mysteries together!" Greg excitedly continued to read newspaper articles, and Marta anxiously continued on with the journal.

"Listen to this." She read aloud from Agatha's journal. "John is angry with me for Johnny's death. He blames me for not watching him closely enough. He doesn't realize how quick Johnny was. Johnny could be happily sitting, playing with toys, and the next minute he would have left the toys and be off in another part of the room. I tried to block him off in a corner with furniture. He would crawl through it. I tried hard to keep him safe. It hurts badly enough to have lost Johnny, without John blaming me. He says such hateful things!"

"That is so sad. They probably didn't have playpens back then," Greg said.

They read on for a short time, when Greg hit on something else. "It says here John Winchell was convicted of the murder of Agatha Brown. He was sentenced to life in prison."

"This box sure is informative. Too bad we didn't stumble across this box the first time we were up there." Marta leaned over and kissed Greg. They had been sitting for hours. "Don't you think it's time for a break, honey?"

"Sweetie, I would love nothing more. I'm afraid if we break we will move on to things we shouldn't, with Maggie here. I'm almost through the newspaper clippings, only a few more. Then we will stop for some lunch. How's that sound?" Greg wanted to keep reading.

"I'd rather have dessert first!" Marta smiled that sly little smile of hers.

Greg chuckled, "You are getting as bad as me!" He then became involved with the clippings again. Minutes later, he screamed. "Mart, you are not going to believe this! He hung himself in prison!"

"Oh my God! John, did?" Marta asked.

"Yes, it says here they found him on morning check, hanging from the bars with a handmade rope, made from pieces of cord that he must have acquired from working in the mail room at the prison." Greg was terribly excited at this point.

"Hmmm, I would have thought he would have been in death row and not allowed out," Marta replied.

"Either they didn't have a death row, or they allowed them out to work. Who knows how things were done back then. Prisons were probably quite primitive back in the early 1900s," Greg stated.

"Now, can we break for lunch? I'm tired of sitting." Marta scooted her chair back, flexed her arms, and stretched her legs.

"Sure, sweetie. Oh my, I have been so involved

here, that I forgot to check on Maggie."

"You didn't see her walk by us and go into the sewing room a while ago?" Marta asked.

"No, I didn't. I guess I was too involved in these clippings. We really have learned a lot this morning. By the way, where is Toto? He was asleep in his bed when we started this."

"He must have followed Maggie into the sewing room." Marta decided.

Sure enough, Toto was on Maggie's lap, as she sat in the wooden rocker in the sewing room. As she rocked, she was reading aloud as if she was reading to someone. Greg decided to ask, "Maggie, honey, are you reading to someone?"

"Yes, Daddy, I'm reading to Johnny. He likes me to read to him."

"Who is Johnny?" Greg was almost afraid to hear the answer.

"He is my little friend, Daddy."

"How old is he? Is he your age?" Greg asked.

"No, Daddy, he is just a baby. He can't even walk yet, he only crawls."

Greg and Marta looked at one another, not knowing what to say next. Greg decided to leave it alone for now. Instead he asked, "Is anyone else in here with you?"

"Grandma is here, too," Maggie revealed.

Greg looked over at Marta. She was just as amazed as he.

Greg then asked, "Is she here often?"

"Yes, she is here almost every day. She talks to me and is really nice to me. I love her."

"Is anyone else here with you?" Greg continued to question.

"Not today, Daddy, but sometimes Johnny's mom, Agatha, is here."

"What does she do when she is here?" Greg was trying to stay calm.

"Not much. She doesn't talk much. She plays with Johnny some of the time. She seems very sad." Maggie appeared to seem sad about this.

"Does your mommy ever come here?" Greg went on.

"Yes, she is here sometimes. She used to be here a lot. Now she can only come once in a while," Maggie calmly stated.

"Why can't she come more often?" Greg asked.

"She is very busy up in heaven. She takes care of the little children who go to heaven. She says they need her, because they are so sad. They have no Mommy or Daddy up there with them. She comes to see me as much as she can. She says I have you and Marta here with me, and the other kids don't have anybody with them."

Greg decided that was enough questions for one day. This was enough to absorb for now. To think there were several spirits in the house was a lot to take in. He and Marta went to the parlor to talk. Lunch no longer seemed important. They had suddenly lost their appetites.

Marta was as stunned as Greg, "What do you think of all that?"

"I knew the house must be haunted. I just had no idea there are so many here. And to think, Lisa's mother is here most every day! And Lisa comes here, too! I did have an idea she had visited at least once." There was now no doubt in Greg's mind that it was Lisa who made passionate love to him, soon after her death, that night on the parlor floor. He had never told Marta about that and didn't really care to share it with her now.

"What made you think she had been here at least once?" Marta questioned.

"I thought I felt her presence one night, that's all." He quickly changed the subject. "What do you think of Agatha being here?"

Marta looked at Greg a little strangely, "I don't know what to think of any of the spirits being here!"

Greg agreed. Somehow he felt most disturbed over Agatha's presence. To think someone who had been murdered so violently was now living under his roof, at least part of the time, caused him to be quite uneasy. It was weird enough to think her baby was in the house and that Maggie spent so much time with him.

Greg shook his head, "Well, we have many of our answers, so what do we do now? I wanted the answers, but I think I feel worse now knowing them. I guess I'm glad that Lisa's mom has been here all along to help Maggie cope with Lisa's death, and I'm glad she has seen Lisa from time to time. The rest of them…we do not need!"

"Greg, sweetie, you say we have many of our answers. Yes, we know who is here, but we still have some mysteries. We know the red, sticky substance appears where two deaths have occurred, but why? And why did it appear in the carriage house? Why was it coming from the trap door? Why did the water in the Jacuzzi turn red like the sticky substance? Why did the portrait of Isadora cry? Why did it flood the bedroom floor? And…with all these spirits, how do we know who raped you?"

Greg thought for a while. "It must have been

Agatha. We can rule out Lisa's mom, and Lisa certainly wouldn't rape me, especially so violently. Somehow, I don't feel it was Isadora. So, that leaves Agatha."

Just then something occurred to Marta. "What if there are even more spirits here?"

"Good God, Mart, don't we have enough here as it is?" Greg sounded almost angry.

"It was just a thought. Sorry, if it upset you."

"The whole thing upsets me! I'm not upset with you. How could I ever be upset with you?"

"Maybe we should talk about something else for a while. This has all been a bit overwhelming. We need to concentrate on something else." Marta was trying to calm him.

"Yeah, like us," Greg smiled that foxy smile of his, and scooted closer to Marta. "That's the closest we have come to arguing. I'm sorry, I shouldn't have snapped at you like that. It's just that it upsets me to think this beautiful old Victorian home, Lisa's and my dream, has become such a fiasco. Lisa loved this house so, and so did I. Now, I don't know what to think. How can it ever be the same? I was planning on calling a realtor today. I couldn't make myself do it. How can I sell Lisa's dream, the last home she lived in? Now, with all we have uncovered, how can I dump these spirits on someone else? What are you smiling about, anyway?"

"I don't mean to be taking this all lightly. Weren't we going to change the subject?" Greg, drew her near, smiled, and began kissing her quite passionately.

"Wow, what a switch!" Marta murmured, as her lips broke away from Greg's before she replanted them on his. The kiss then became quite intense.

"Careful, sweetie, Maggie is here and probably getting hungry by now," Greg warned.

"I almost forgot. And something else I almost forgot. I'm meeting a client at three. I really have to scoot soon, as much as I hate to." Marta looked disappointed.

"No more than I hate for you to leave. Tomorrow is our big night at The Towers. Don't forget!" Greg teased.

"Don't worry about that, there is no way I will forget that!"

They went to the kitchen and scrounged up lunch. Maggie was quite hungry. She wolfed it down and ran upstairs to check on Dorothy, with Toto on her heels.

"At least she didn't go back into the sewing room. That's a plus!" Greg said.

"I hate to say it, but it's time for me to leave, honey," Marta reminded Greg.

Greg wrapped his arms around her and kissed her as if they would be separated for months. He missed her even before she left the drive.

Eleven

The long awaited night at The Towers had arrived. Greg, handsome, sexy and looking quite distinguished in a black tux, rang Marta's doorbell. She answered the door, absolutely gorgeous in her sleek, black, spaghetti strap dress, which showed her deep cleavage. Her hair was styled in a fancy up do, with long wisps accentuating her lovely face. Once Greg caught his breath, it was all he could do to keep from making love to her right there. He wondered how he could make it through the evening without at least reaching in and touching her breasts.

"What a way to start an evening!" he thought to himself. Instead, he held his tongue and said something more appropriate. "Hi, Sweetie, you look gorgeous!"

Marta gleamed, "Why, thank you. You look quite handsome yourself!"

Greg put his arms around her, and gave her a warm, lasting kiss, which she of course returned, careful not to smudge her bronzine lipstick.

The Towers was at full capacity, as usual for New Year's Eve, this being the finest and most elegant place in town. There must have been two hundred couples, all richly dressed in elegant gowns and tuxes. The evening began with an exquisite meal of lobster, served with a special sauce only served at The Towers. It was a rare occasion that Greg or Marta had lobster. It was especially pricey at The Towers, as everything was. Tonight was quite special for Marta and Greg; as it was their first formal date. Greg had definitely gone all out for this New Year's Eve. Was this telling Marta what to expect in the days ahead?

The evening was invitingly romantic with a full orchestra to dance to. This was the first Greg and Marta had danced together. Greg was amazed at how well Marta danced. She led at first, until he caught on. He was being taken in by her...he was definitely falling in love with her. He held her closely, so closely he could feel her heart racing. Her magnificent breasts were warm and delightful against his chest. Her bare backed dress, his hand touching her skin, gave rise to even more emotion. It had been a long time since he had felt such emotions. Greg knew she felt the same way. Neither regretted when the evening at The Towers concluded, as they were both anxious to express their love for one another.

When they drove into the drive it was dark. They were too aroused to have noticed the dark cloud that enveloped the house, even if it had been light out. Greg fumbled with the key in the front door lock. He couldn't think about anything else, other than making love to Marta. They made it to the spiral staircase before they began ripping off their own clothes—this seemed to be the quickest way. When Greg was down to his black, bikini briefs, it was quite obvious to Marta they no longer contained his erection. She thought she would orgasm just looking at him. He unfastened her black, satin bra, threw it on the staircase, laid her on the floor, and quickly removed her black, satin panties. There was no foreplay needed—thoughts on the dance floor had taken care of that. He tore his briefs off and quickly entered her. She was equally aroused and came even before he entered her. She was almost out of control from the start, screaming for more, wanting to be driven higher and higher. It was over almost before it started.

"Wow, what just happened?" Greg was out of breath, smiling that cocky smile of his.

"Wow, is right. Suppose we had too much to drink?" Marta wondered aloud.

"It never gave me that kind of rush before!" he laughed. "It was great though!"

They climbed the spiral staircase to the bedroom. It wasn't over yet—after all, they had skipped the foreplay. Greg joked, "I want some afterplay!" And that they had! They kissed, sucked and tasted for quite some time. Marta was being taken higher than ever before. Greg didn't know it was possible for a woman to orgasm so many times in one night. Once the fire died down some within them, they kissed warmly, and dozed off awhile. When they awoke, they again made love—gently and affectionately—holding, touching, and kissing. They both felt this was the turning point of their relationship. They knew it was now much more than just sex. Greg cradled Marta in his arms all through the night while they slept.

Toward morning, Greg awoke to the terrible stench. He opened his eyes to find the red substance had flooded the floor. He awakened Marta, and they quickly threw on some clothes. As they ran out the bedroom door, Greg caught a glimpse of the Jacuzzi. It was bubbling rapidly with the blood-like substance overflowing down the sides of the tub. When they got to the hall, they could see it was also flowing down the spiral staircase. The grand drawing room floor, and possibly the floor of the entire house was flooded with the red stuff. Greg's keys were in the pocket of his trousers, which had been left on the floor by the staircase. His trousers now must be under the red substance, as they were nowhere to be seen. He reached his hands into the substance and felt around for his trousers. He grabbed hold of the trousers and felt for the pocket. Once he located the pocket, he felt inside— there were no keys there. He and Marta both groped through the blood-like substance searching for them. Finally, Greg's hand snagged onto them. He took Marta's hand and they fled out the front door.

He wiped the keys off on his clothes and inserted them into the ignition. The Tahoe failed to start. Greg was panicking. He again wiped the keys off—it fired, only to die. Again, he wiped the keys, almost dropping them on the floor. He was shaking so badly, he couldn't guide the key into the ignition. "Please, God," he pleaded. The key went in. He gave it a turn. Finally, it started. Driving erratically, he fled the driveway not knowing where he was headed. One thing he did know was that he was not going back to that haunted house. Eerie things had occurred before. Greg felt this time was different—whatever it was in that house was trying to end their lives.

How could his and Lisa's dream home have gone so wrong? Marta was sobbing, becoming more and more frightened by Greg's reckless driving. It was snowing, and the roads were slick. She couldn't get him to come to his senses and slow down. The Tahoe went off the road and began sliding down a steep embankment, picking up speed as it traveled. It flipped over, landed upside down, and continued on down the hillside until it hit a tree. It then flipped over on its side, pinning Greg in. Marta was knocked unconscious. When she came to, she was confused as to what had happened. Greg was lifeless, his head buried in the air bag. There was blood everywhere...blood and the red substance from the house, which was all over them from searching for the keys. "Oh, my God, he's dead!" she thought. She unfastened her seat belt and reached over to feel for a pulse. It was weak, but he was alive. Her purse was now hanging from the rear view mirror, flung there from the crash. She reached in and clutched her cell phone fumbling to call 911.

At that moment, she realized a man on OnStar was talking. "Can anyone hear me? Mr. Carrington, are you okay? An ambulance is on its way."

At the same time, a voice from her cell phone was saying, "Can I help you? Is there a problem?" The lady on the other end of the cell phone could hear OnStar saying an ambulance was on its way. She was grateful to hear this, as she had no idea where Marta was calling from, and Marta was of no help. Marta was quite shaken and didn't know where they were.

The ambulance soon arrived. It was difficult for the paramedics to reach them, as the embankment was extremely steep. They radioed for help when they saw how far down the embankment the vehicle was. The Jaws of Life was needed to free Greg. By the time he was freed, valuable time had been lost. He had lost a great amount of blood.

Marta had reluctantly been placed in an ambulance. She overheard one of the paramedics say, "This looks bad; this guy will be lucky if he makes it to the hospital."

Marta began to scream hysterically and passed out. When she came to, she was in the hospital. No one would tell her anything. She couldn't see Greg anywhere. *Oh, my God,* she thought. *He's dead.*

About that time, she heard the shrill of an ambulance siren, and overheard a nurse say, "They're bringing in the guy that was with her. He's just barely hanging on."

Marta was relieved to know he was alive, but at the same time she was terribly scared she would lose him. She asked a nurse what his injuries were and was told only that the doctors were with him, working to stabilize him. Marta had multiple cuts and bruises with possible broken ribs. She needed x-rays and a cat scan, since she had passed out twice. She lay there for what seemed like hours, when she heard Lori's voice asking where Greg Carrington and Marta Thornton were.

"She's in cubicle three, just around the corner. He's in four. They're still trying to stabilize him," the lady at the desk replied.

Just as Lori entered the cubicle where Marta was, a voice came over the loud speaker "Code blue in four".

"Oh, my God, that's Greg," screamed Lori and Marta, together.

Greg saw himself lying in the emergency room as if he was looking down from above.

"Oh, my...that guy down there looks a lot like me." He watched as a man in a white lab coat rushed to the guy's side. The man had paddles in his hand, like the ones he had seen in movies, when someone's heart stops. "Oh, my God, that's me down there. I must be dead!" Just then, Greg felt himself moving rapidly down a long dark tunnel. A light appeared at the end of the tunnel. In the light, he saw two figures, one heavenly figure, which he soon realized was Lisa.

Another, standing beside Lisa, was a Christ-like figure, which spoke. "I brought you here for a reason. Lisa is here to explain some things to you. When she is finished, you must go back. It is not your time."

"Hi, sweetie," Lisa looked radiant and totally at peace. "Greg, honey, you can't stay. Maggie needs you and so does Marta. You have made me so happy that you and Marta have fallen in love. This is what I have been praying for. What you don't know is that I have been guiding you to her, making this happen. I know you have felt you were betraying me and that you shouldn't be doing this. You couldn't help it, because I'm making it happen—for you and for Maggie. Thinking back, don't you think it was unlike you to be so strongly attracted to her in the beginning? I may have overdone it a bit. I'm hoping for the two of you to marry—for the three of you to be a family.

There is more you need to know…about the house. You and Marta have been quite the detectives I see. There are some things you haven't been able to find the answers for. I can help you with that, because I see all. First of all, there is Isadora, the daughter of the Stephens'. Yes, she is the one in the portrait. She cries, as she is very sad. She refuses to accept that she is dead. She has remained in the house. She died so young that she never had a relationship with a man. Because of this, she feels she has been cheated. She thought when I died she could have you for herself. She came to you when you were sleeping, and I guess you could say, she raped you. Now that you have found Marta and have made love with her, you have angered Isadora. Have you noticed that every time you and Marta make love, something bad happens? You angered her terribly last night when the two of you made such passionate love. She got together with Agatha and caused the house to be flooded with that horrible red, substance.

Remember, Agatha is the one Maggie told you sometimes visits her and plays with her son, little Johnny. I see you have uncovered all the mysteries concerning she and Johnny. She is still very sad over all that happened. She left the house after her death and was buried behind the house where you now have your garden. Her remains are deep under your garden; nonetheless—you disturbed her, and she has returned to haunt you. It is she that you have seen as a streak of light coming and going between her grave and the house—and throughout the house. She has haunted you with the blood-like substance in the hallway where she was killed, on the mansard stairs where Johnny died, and in the carriage house where John kept her body while he dug her grave.

It was Isadora you recently saw off the kitchen, when you thought it was me. I don't make myself visible to you, because it would only set you back. You need to keep moving forward with Marta.

Greg, honey, I watch you always. I long to be with you, although I am happy here. I am happy that you and Marta have found each other. I need nothing more. I must tell you, though—when I first died—I wanted to return to be with you. In fact, I did return once—and made love with you—on the floor in front of the fireplace. You felt it might have been me, and that pleased me. It was wonderful, Greg. I just had to have you...one last time. Please, don't confuse it with the time you dreamed you had violent sex. That was Isadora.

I was there when you cut down the Christmas tree. I couldn't miss the cutting of our first blue spruce. It is good that I was there, because I was able to pull Maggie from the falling tree. I know you felt it was me, not her guardian angel, as you suggested to Maggie.

Greg, sweetie, don't let Isadora or Agatha scare you. They mean you no harm, or anyone else in the house. They only mean to haunt you. It is safe to go back to the house now. As always before, the red, sticky substance is gone. You need to rid the house of Isadora and Agatha. You should ask them to leave. Tell them they need to go to the light. If they remain, perhaps you should consult a psychic medium, although I feel that won't be necessary. I will talk to Mom and see if she thinks Maggie will be okay now, if she should leave. I know she has helped Maggie adjust to my death. I have visited Maggie, not often, as I think she will do better if I am not with her all the time. Besides, I am busy helping the lonely and confused little children up here, just as I told Maggie. I will let you decide what to do about Johnny. He is company for Maggie, but after all, he is a spirit. I would suggest you consult a psychiatrist, although in a case like this he would probably laugh at you.

You must go now, sweetie. I love you dearly and always will. God is telling me you must go back. Know that I will be with you always, even from up here. Someday you will come to stay, and we will be together again for all eternity. Do not rush this—enjoy your life on earth with Marta and Maggie. As for me…time is different up here. It goes so very fast—like flashes."

She hugged Greg. He kissed her warmly, almost passionately, not wanting to leave her. He could see the doctors with the paddles. He opened his eyes. He was no longer looking down. He was back—alive. He wondered—had he dreamed he talked to Lisa? No, he knew he had really spoken to her. He remembered everything she had said.

He could now hear the doctors talking.

"His pressure is coming up. He is starting to stabilize."

Greg wasn't concerned about himself. God had told him that it was not his time. He now remembered Marta had been in the car with him. "Marta, is she okay?"

No one was answering him. He became agitated. Just then Lori entered the cubicle. She was relieved to see he was alive.

He repeated, "Mart…is she okay?"

Lori reassured him that her injuries were only minor and that she would be okay.

Soon Marta was wheeled to his bedside. This calmed him, seeing for himself that she was okay. He reached his hand out to her, unable to hug her as he wanted to.

The doctors reassured Marta that Greg would be fine now. He was receiving blood to replace all that he had lost. He had a bad gash on his head and had sliced his leg badly. An artery had been severed. Therefore, he had lost a substantial amount of blood before the paramedic's arrived. This artery was now repaired, as was the gash in his head and the leg laceration.

Marta was wheeled off for a CAT scan. The x-rays had shown no broken ribs. Now it was necessary to rule out any head injury. The doctor had wanted her to lie still until after the CAT scan. She insisted on seeing Greg. She had heard the code blue and would not rest until she had seen him.

Greg was told only that she needed to rest. He was preoccupied with having seen Lisa. He could hardly believe he had actually talked to her. She looked so beautiful, almost like an angel—she had a glow around her, although she was in somewhat of a human form. He fell asleep wondering how he could tell Marta, without her thinking he wanted Lisa and not her.

When he awoke, Marta was out of the CAT scan and had been told they had found nothing unusual. She would stay overnight for observation and would probably be allowed to go home the next day.

Even though Greg had stabilized, he was still extremely weak from the blood loss. They found a room for him and were keeping a close watch on him. Marta was put in a room across the hall. She lay rethinking all that had taken place in a short time. The perfectly wonderful night at The Towers had gone bad—quickly. Greg had seemed different, so much closer and more in love. She felt their love had taken a big step forward—then, to have almost lost him. She had been terribly frightened and was wondering what she would have done without him now...after finally getting together with him after all the years of loving him and not being able to share that love with him. She wouldn't dwell on this. He would be okay now, and they would be together.

The next morning, Marta was told she could go home. She was reluctant to leave Greg. She called Lori. Lori convinced her she should go home. She would be there soon to give her a ride. Meanwhile, Marta went in to see Greg again. He looked much better than the night before. The doctor had said he might even go home the next day. Marta hugged him. As tears flowed from her eyes, she said, "I love you, sweetie. You know that, don't you?"

"Of course I do, Mart. I feel the same way. I love you very much. When I get home, we will have a long talk."

By now, Lori had arrived with Maggie. They were looking for Marta in her room. Maggie saw Marta and Greg across the hall and went running, "Daddy, Daddy, are you okay?"

"Sure, sweetheart, I'm fine, just a little sore and weak right now. Soon, I'll be good as new."

She hugged Marta, "I'm glad you are okay, too. You know I love you like a mommy!"

Greg and Marta were both surprised to hear these words come out of her mouth. They were so fortunate to have found this new love—one that Maggie seemed to share.

Twelve

While Greg was recuperating, he thought long and hard about how to rid the house of the spirits. He asked Steve to come over. He needed to talk to him. Greg greeted him at the door.

"More spirit problems, have we?" Steve asked.

"Actually, they have been fairly quiet lately—only a few flashes of light. Agatha paces the halls, I guess."

"Agatha? The spirits have names now?"

"That's what I want to talk to you about. It's a rather long story. Come sit here in the kitchen. I have some things to show you first." Greg poured coffee for the two of them. "How about a sweet roll?"

"No, thanks, I just ate. So what do you want to show me?"

Greg placed the box from the mansard on the table, took several clippings from it, and placed them on the table along with Agatha's journal. "Before the accident, Marta and I found some answers to the mysteries of this house…quite interesting. This house has a lot of history… history that I could do without."

Greg showed Steve each of the articles and read the coinciding entries in the journal. When he was finished, Steve, astonished, sat back in his chair, "This is absolutely amazing! To think these spirits are here with us now."

"Yeah, tell me about it! There's more Steve."

"Christ, Greg, isn't this enough?"

Greg proceeded to explain, "When I was in the ER after my accident, I actually left this world for a short time."

Steve was speechless.

Greg continued, "I saw Lisa."

"Oh, my! Really? How could that be?"

"I saw myself lying on a bed in the ER. It was as if I was floating above, looking down. I saw a doctor approach me with paddles. I felt myself going through a tunnel toward a light. I moved very swiftly, it seemed. In the light I saw a Christ like figure and Lisa, so radiant she almost glowed."

"Holy shit!" Steve was astonished.

Greg continued to tell him what he was told by the Christ like figure, and what Lisa said.

"Totally, totally amazing!" Steve could hardly believe what he was hearing.

"This brings me to something I want to ask of you, Steve."

"And what might that be?"

"I have decided to do as Lisa suggested. I want to ask Isadora and Agatha to leave. I first need to convince Isadora that she is dead."

"Oh, this should be real interesting!" Steve chuckled. "And when do you propose to do this?"

"Whenever you can help me." Greg was hoping Steve would agree to help.

"Oh, how did I know this was coming! You want me to be here when you tell Isadora she is dead...and ask her and Agatha to leave?"

"Yes, will you do it?" Greg asked.

"You think it will work?"

"Who knows—we've got to try something."

"I love that we part," Steve grinned.

"Well, will you help?"

"Sure, what are brothers-in-law for, if it isn't to help each other out? We guys need to stick together. What about Marta, will she be here?" Steve asked.

"I'd rather she not be. Knowing her, she will insist on being here. I haven't gotten into any of this with her, yet. I've had a lot to think about since the accident."

"I guess you have," Steve agreed.

"I'll talk to Mart today. Could you come over tomorrow morning? Maggie will be in school."

"Sure, there's nothing on my slate for tomorrow."

"Great, I need to get this taken care of and get back to work. By the way, did you see my new car in the drive? Mart and I went shopping."

"Yeah, a bit sporty for an old guy like you, don't you think? I figured you'd get another Tahoe."

"I planned to, then I saw this Porsche and figured it might spice things up a bit around here. I've always had a bit of a thing for a red sports car." Greg looked pleased with himself.

"Is it the new 997?" Steve inquired, excitedly?

"It sure is!"

"I've read about them and have seen a picture of one, but I hadn't actually seen one yet. I wasn't even sure they were out yet."

"This is the first one the dealership has gotten in. I think the dealer almost hated to see it go. They are difficult to get right now, since they are so new."

"Wow…how exciting! What's Marta think of it?"

"She loves it! Something tells me when we get

married she will fight me for it. I'll probably wind up driving her jeep."

"Did I hear the word married?"

"You caught that, did you?"

"Sure did!"

"Just wanted to see your reaction! I'm considering asking her to marry me. Heck, I might as well. It's going to happen anyway with Lisa up there running the show! Seriously, Steve, I've fallen in love with her. I never thought I could love another woman after Lisa died, especially so soon, but I guess Lisa has seen to that. Marta is a wonderful gal. She makes me happy again. When I'm with her, I can almost forget the past. And…she turns me on immensely! I need her in my life. When she isn't with me, I can't wait until we are together again."

"Sounds like love to me. You have my blessings. Lori and I think a lot of her, too. I know Lori will be excited to hear this."

"Hey, mums the word until I ask Marta!" Greg insisted.

"You got it!" They shook hands and Steve was off.

Greg was nervous about Marta coming over. He hadn't told her he had talked to Lisa. He had needed to keep it to himself for a while to sort through his feelings.

Marta arrived, all bubbly, wanting to be with Greg. They were like a couple of teenagers—with just a bit more maturity.

They went to the parlor. When they were finished snuggling and kissing, Greg looked Marta directly in the eye.

"Sweetie, before we get too involved here, we need to talk. There is something I haven't told you, something that happened when I was in the ER. Mart, you know I coded?"

"Yes, honey, I was so scared. I thought I was losing you."

"You did, for a few moments. I actually died for a very short time.

Marta gasped, "What? How do you know that?"

"I saw Lisa."

"Oh my gosh…really?"

Greg proceeded to explain.

Marta was in awe. "That is totally remarkable!"

"It certainly is. I've had a lot of time to think about it. Not only did I see her and talk to her; she also gave me the answers to the mysteries we were unable to piece together. It was a lot for me to absorb. Forgive me, for not sharing it with you right away. I needed time."

While explaining this to Marta, he suddenly remembered the night when he and Marta had sex in the kitchen. After Marta had mentioned he should have locked the door—and he hadn't—had Lisa locked the door? Had she instigated that and locked the door so no one would see them? Suddenly, Marta interrupted his thoughts.

"I understand, sweetie. Does this change anything between us?"

"No, baby, I still love you very much. Lisa was my past. You are my present." He took her in his arms, and held her tightly. They kissed, lovingly…tenderly. Greg drew back, still keeping her close. "I have asked Steve to come over in the morning to help me ask Isadora and Agatha to leave."

"Really? What time should I be here?"

"Marta, I don't want you here. We don't know

how the spirits will react. They could cause a lot of havoc. I don't want to put you in any danger."

"You aren't serious! You think I will stay away? Nothing doing! I will be by your side!"

Greg knew better than to go any further with this. Her mind was made up.

*

The next morning Steve pulled into the drive behind Marta. Greg greeted them at the door. "Are the two of you ready for this?"

"Ready as I'll ever be," they laughed, as they spoke in unison.

Greg had candles lit in the kitchen and the servants' hallway.

"What are the candles for?" Steve asked.

"Not sure. Something told me candles might help. I had them here, so I thought I would use them."

Marta wasn't so sure.

Greg began to speak, his hands trembling, "Isadora, if you are here, please, listen. You must know you are no longer alive. You died a long long time ago when you got sick with tuberculosis. You must go toward the light. This is my home now. I do not need you. Go now—and leave us alone. Go toward the light. You will be happy there. You will never find happiness here, as we do not want you here." He paused as if he was listening for an answer. Then he proceeded. "Agatha, I know you are here. I am sorry I disturbed you. You must go now. Go toward the light. You can take Johnny with you. We do not want or need you here. Please leave at once."

Steve and Marta were surprised at the simplicity of

his speech. They felt this would do no good. Suddenly the house became dark, as if it was again engulfed in a dark cloud. The candles began to flicker, then went out. The kitchen sink began to make a bubbling sound. Marta and Greg were familiar with the sound—and the stench. There were streaks of light—inside and out—flashes everywhere. The house began to shake. There were moaning and crying sounds and rumbles as if it was thundering. The streaks of light seemed to be going from one room to another, as if someone was running through the house in terror.

Greg, Marta, and Steve all held hands. They didn't know what to think or do. Should they run from the house—or stand still? Suddenly, as they stood holding hands, the house quit shaking. The moans, cries, and rumbling stopped. The house lit up again. There was total calm, not even a whisper of wind—only silence. When the house lit up Marta caught a glimpse of the last of the red substance going down the drain. No one moved for fear it would all start again.

Finally, after what seemed like hours, which had only been a few minutes, Greg asked, "Well, what do you think?"

"That was damn scary, is what I think," Steve still appeared stunned.

"Do you think that's the end of it?" Marta asked, trembling and looking a bit pale.

Greg put his arm around Marta, "Hard to tell, all we can do is hope for the best."

Steve decided he'd had enough excitement for one day. "Let me know if anything more happens," and he was out the door, headed home.

*

214

Marta and Greg went to the parlor and put on some music. He held her closely, as they listened to "If There Hadn't Been You," sung by Billy Dean.

When the song finished playing, Greg spoke up, "Sweetie, how about if we get away for a night, and take a break from this house and all the memories, good and bad."

"That sounds really wonderful, honey."

"Would tonight be too soon? That is, if Steve and Lori can watch Maggie."

"That's great with me, sweetie. The sooner the better."

Greg phoned Lori. She said she would love to have Maggie overnight. She could run her to school the next morning. Greg then dialed the Eagle Inn and Resort there in Galena and reserved a suite for the night.

"I guess I had better go home and pack a few things and cancel an appointment with a client for tomorrow morning." Marta was getting anxious.

"I hate to see you leave so soon. Got time for a quickie?" Greg winked.

Marta laughed. "I know you're just teasing. Besides, I don't think I'm ready to test the spirits quite yet. I will accept for tonight though, and I don't mean for a quickie." She put her arms around Greg and held him tightly. He could tell she didn't want to leave just yet. Her good-bye kiss showed that. Marta softly and regretfully said, "I had better get going, before we test the spirits." She reluctantly drove off.

Maggie was delighted to be able to go to the farm. She immediately began packing up Dorothy and Toto. Greg helped her pack a bag so she would have appropriate clothes for school. He called Marta to see how soon she would be ready.

"I've been packed and ready for an hour now."

Greg chuckled, "Okay, Maggie is home and raring to go. I will be there in a few minutes—or would you rather I drop her off first?"

"No, sweetie, come get me first. I can't stand being away from you another minute."

Greg chuckled again. He knew how she felt. He felt the same way. Steve greeted them at the door of the farmhouse, "Well? Anything, yet?"

"No, all is quiet," Greg, answered.

Steve teased, "So, why you leaving then? Scared?"

"We just wanted some time away. We're going over to Eagle Inn."

"Oh, I got it. For some romance, huh?"

Greg smiled and went off to find Maggie. She and Toto had gone looking for Tinker Bell. He gave Maggie a hug and told her he would see her after school the next day.

As they drove off in the new, red Porsche, Lori thought what a cute couple they made. Lisa had known what she was doing.

"What do you want to do about supper, sweetie? Do you want to stop somewhere to eat first?"

"I'm not really thinking about food right now. What do you want to do?" He winked.

Marta knew what that meant.

"I guess we'll worry about that later. We will eventually get hungry."

The room was even more impressive than Greg had expected. He had heard from others how cozy and romantic the suites were, with fireplaces and Jacuzzis. The fireplace was already lit when they arrived. Greg placed some pillows on the floor in front of the fireplace and put on some music—"I'll Go on Loving You", sung by Alan Jackson. Greg lay down on one pillow and invited Marta to join him. Wine was chilling on the hearth. He poured two glasses and handed one to Marta. He made a toast, "To us baby!" They listened to the music, as they sipped wine, feeling more romantic with each gentle touch—each kiss.

Greg looked directly into Marta's eyes, "Marta, sweetie, will you marry me?" With these words, he reached over and took her left hand. He placed a 1.25-carat solitaire diamond ring on the tip of her ring finger and waited for her answer.

"Oh, yes, sweetie, yes, yes!" With this, he slid the sparkling, diamond ring on her finger.

They kissed, passionately, knowing their love would be forever…as long as their forever might be.

Epilogue

Greg and Marta were married six months later. It has been one year since that fabulous night at the Eagle Inn when Greg placed the ring on Marta's finger. Their love remains as fresh and vibrant as it was that night.

Life at the Carrington Victorian home is much different now. There have been no signs of Isadora and Agatha since the day Greg asked them to leave. There have not been any streaks of light, or any red, sticky substance, or any crying portraits. There also are no cries of a baby. Greg assumes that Agatha took Johnny with her.

Greg had Agatha's remains moved to a nearby cemetery. He searched and found a grave in this cemetery with a marker that read, Johnny Brown, infant son of Agatha Brown. It is here beside this small grave, where Agatha's remains now rest.

Lisa's mom appears to come and go. Maggie has adjusted well. She spends much of her time with Toto and has become more interested in her little friends, Kaitlyn and Amy. A few new friends have also come her way. She is now very excited that she soon will have a new baby brother or sister. Marta and Greg will be sure it's not named after a fairy tale...as how appropriate would a name like Tinker Bell or Toto be for a baby!

Marta is now four months pregnant and just beginning to show. She is even more beautiful; that certain glow of pregnancy is apparent. Greg is thrilled with the prospect of a new baby on the way. He isn't a bit unhappy with Marta's enlarging breasts. He can hardly keep his eyes off them. Their sex life is...well...you can imagine! Greg cherishes each and every moment they have together, as he now knows how precious life is. Lisa remains in their memories and in their hearts, as she was so very special to them both.

Callie Norse

As an avid reader, Callie Norse has dreamed of being a published author since junior high. After raising her three children, she developed a short story concept into the book she had always dreamed of writing. After readers showed much enthusiasm over this book, she was prompted to make this the first in the Carrington series. She resides in Illinois with her husband, and continues to write. You can visit her at http://www.callienorse.com.

Thank you for reading my book. If you enjoyed it, would you please take a minute to leave me a review at your favorite retailer? I would love to hear your comments about this book. If you wish to do so, you can email me at callienorse@yahoo.com.

You may also join me at:
http://www.facebook.com/callie.norse
http://www.twitter.com/callienorse

The Carrington Series consists of:
1. For the Love of Lisa
2. A Love Too Soon
3. The Anniversary…not to be forgotten
4. Flashes from the Past

This series goes on throughout many years as they age. The books can be read separately, if one wishes, as there is some backstory in each.